ANYWHERE BUT HOME
Copyright © 2025 by Brittni DeRiggi

ISBN: 979-8-9922605-9-5

Cover Design by Brittany Evans @BEDESIGNS.CA

Edited and Formatted by Represent Publishing

Anywhere
But
Home

Anywhere But Home

BRITTNI DERIGGI

Represent Publishing

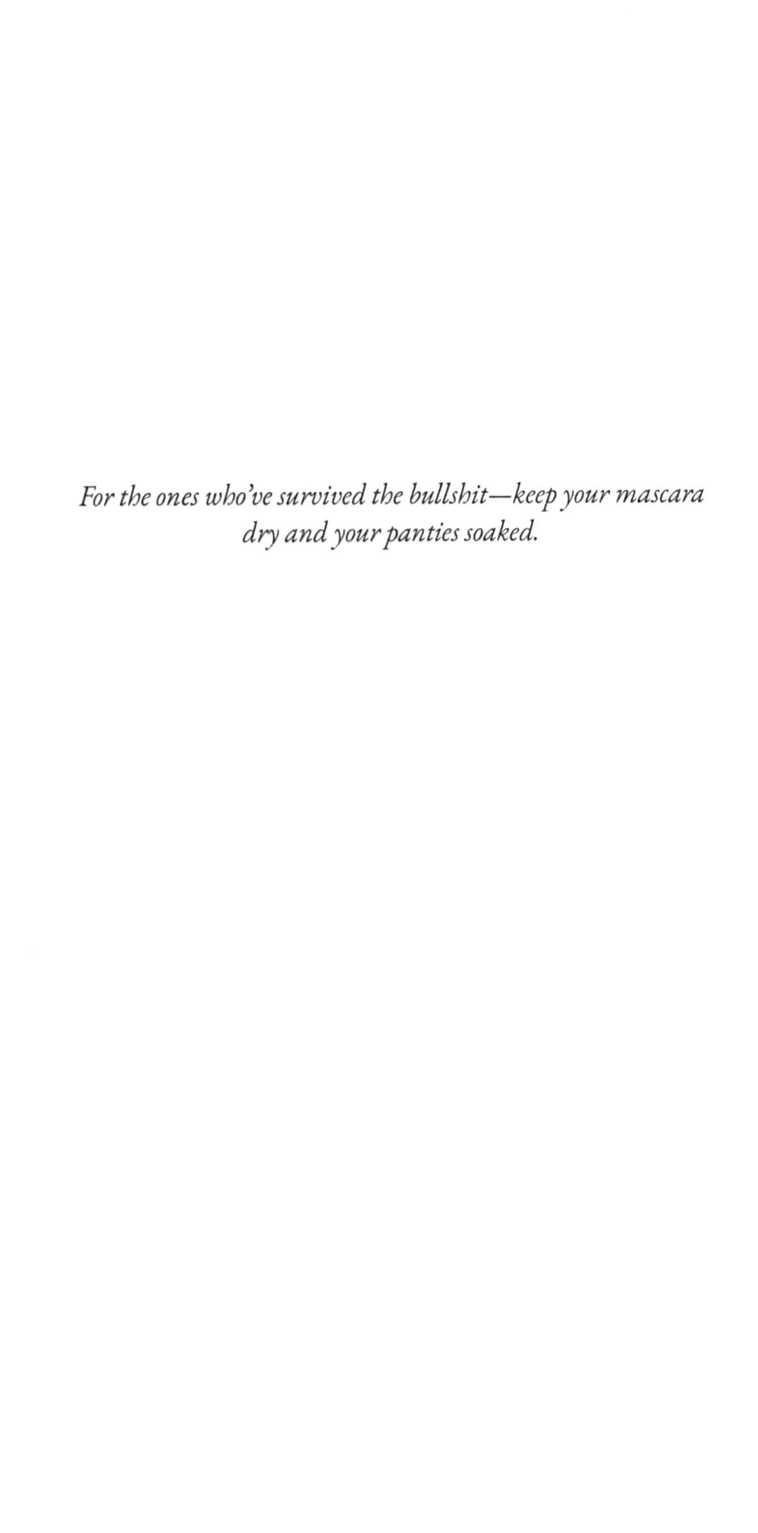

For the ones who've survived the bullshit—keep your mascara dry and your panties soaked.

Trigger Warnings

This book is not just rainbows, sunshine, and dick. It is messy. It is real, and sometimes it hurts.

Inside, you will find mentions of:

- Domestic violence
- Miscarriage
- Line of duty death

If any of that feels too heavy, shut the book, walk away, come back later—or don't. Your peace matters more than any book. If you're still here, turn the page and welcome to this storm.

National Domestic Violence Hotline
Call: 800-799-7233
Text: BEGIN to 88788
Website: thehotline.org

Chapter One
Haylee

When I came home last night to my NYC apartment, I had found everything in disarray and most of my belongings broken, as if someone had placed my apartment in a snow globe and shaken it with force.

My lamp was thrown into the television, magazines scattered on the floor, glass from every picture frame shattered across the area rug. An entire shelf that displayed my collection of vinyls knocked over. Every room in the apartment matched a similar description.

I know exactly who did it: Paul.

He had left bread crumbs. Literally. I mean, who commits a B&E and steals nothing but a sandwich?

He had left the loaf of bread out with crumbs all over the counter. It still irks me all the same now as it did two months ago when he still held the title *boyfriend*.

Even without crumbs coating the countertop and a knife of mayo laid across the cutting board, I knew it was him. He's been a nightmare since I ended our five-year relationship.

I had poured myself a glass of cabernet and sat on the

floor, taking in the view of my broken belongings as tears streaked my face. Then, after the much needed sulking session, I spent two hours on a bench in Central Park, then another two putting my apartment back together.

I keep trying to put all the pieces together as to why.

To scare me?

To let me know he still has all the power?

I know he's unstable, but why break in? I never thought he would take it this far. Then again, I never thought he would threaten my life, either.

Once I was settled last night, I decided to get the hell out of the city. I'd had enough. I needed a break from feeling like his eyes were on me. It's nerve-racking. So, I emailed my boss that I would be taking the week off. Then I booked a one-way ticket to visit my sister in Canyon Falls, Texas.

He might still find me, but at least it will give me time to breathe instead of dealing with being stalked and harassed day in and day out. It has only gotten more extreme as the days passed. The comfort of being at the office and at home has quickly dwindled. I am constantly looking over my shoulder; the feeling of pins and needles shooting up my spine every time I step foot out the door.

At this point, I'm not even sure if he would give a shit if someone saw him lay a hand on me. I'd changed every detail of my normal routine, even down to when I come and go to places like work and my usual coffee spot. I had thought the best option was to avoid him entirely. Though I can't help but question my decision to place all his crap outside the front door and change the locks.

I hadn't wanted to come face-to-face with him again after what happened. I figured any man would eventually just move on.

Not Paul.

Apparently, Paul doesn't just move on.

Most people would have gotten a restraining order or called the police, but I rendered that pointless long ago. He thinks I belong to him—like I'm his possession; his property. It also doesn't help that he thinks I'm going to come running back into his arms. Just like I have every other time.

The first and last time I contacted the police was when Paul had a little too much to drink after what was supposed to be a relaxing night in. I wanted to watch a movie, curl up on the couch, and drink a bottle of my favorite red wine.

But, no.

He had pulled out the scotch.

It was all downhill from there. By the time I spoke with the 911 operator, Paul forced the phone from my hand and hung up. When the police arrived, the officer fist bumped Paul.

I should've known better.

Paul Phillips is one of NYPD's finest.

He explained to the officer that the black eye and cut on my face were from bending down in the freezer and hitting my face on the corner of the refrigerator door I hadn't shut.

Asshole.

He told them I was being dramatic, that I didn't need medical attention and all was fine. He even made a lame joke that even the fridge didn't think I needed ice cream.

Asshole.

I shouldn't have called the police. Not only because I knew once they walked out the door a black eye was the least of my problems, but my word meant nothing over an officer's, who's been on the force for over a decade.

He spent the next several weeks apologizing, sending me flowers and gifts. Hell, he bought me a diamond bracelet.

I forgave him.

Time and time again.

I had already dedicated so much time to our relationship

at that point. A man I once loved and trusted. Now, I look back on it as nothing but weakness. Once turned into twice, which turned into more times than I can count. There were countless apologies, gifts, and flowers. Jesus, once he broke my arm and we went to Cancun.

I'm so goddamn stupid. I mean, who forgives someone for that?

This time, *I'm done*.

This time, I am *not* going back.

As for the last time Paul laid his hands on me, well, that was much different. I'd never seen the look in his eyes like I had that night. The crazed expression plastered across his face and him holding a loaded gun to my head.

Unfortunately, that was what it took for me to realize I needed to get the hell out. In a way, I am grateful that his actions finally led to something clicking in my head, even if it was the sound of a gun cocking at my temple.

Chapter Two
Haylee

I am finally walking off the tarmac and all I can think is, *thank god I'm free*. One might think my sense of freedom is from finally feeling safer than I have in months. They'd be right if it wasn't for the man that had sat next to me on the flight, who smelled like rotting garbage. I had breathed out of my mouth the entire flight, wondering how someone wound up smelling as bad as he did.

Maybe a hoarder?

A garbage man?

A lingering infection?

Maybe the intolerable smell was a good distraction, because now, without it, my mind wanders back to that night. I can almost smell the alcohol and cigarettes coming from Paul's breath.

Focus, Haylee.

He's not here.

Not yet.

I roll my eyes, making my way to my luggage. I breathe in the stuffy airport air, trying to forget all my problems.

Though, my mind jumps back to the smack across my face. The feel of cold steel pressed against my temple. The sound of the gun cracked against my skull.

Stop.

You're safe.

A hand touches my arm, and I jump, sucking all the air into my lungs. A shiver running down my spine as my pulse echoes in my head.

"Excuse me, ma'am," a man with a handlebar mustache says, leaning in for his luggage at the baggage carousel. I exhale at the sound of the unfamiliar voice.

It's just a man with a Hulk Hogan mustache.

It's not him.

But, shit.

I need to fuckin' relax.

I spot my Louis Vuitton luggage making its way toward me on the conveyor belt, and I weave in and out of travelers. My flight was longer than estimated due to a storm in New York, and I have to hustle. I can only imagine how long my ride has been waiting.

Just as I walk toward the exit, my phone vibrates from my back pocket. The screen lights up with my sister's name.

ALYSSA

I STILL haven't gotten it.

HAYLEE

Didn't you take a test?

ALYSSA

No. What if I do and it's not positive?

HAYLEE

It's going to happen!

I am just walking out of the airport to meet your cottage boy.

> I'll make him stop, I'll grab a test, and we
> can do it together.

ALYSSA

> His name is Knox and he's not a boy. He
> bought the cottage a year ago. You really
> need to stop calling him that.

I laugh at my sister's text. Not fully understanding the dynamic of which she, my brother-in-law, and Knox all cohabitate on their property.

Alyssa moved from New York City to a small town in Texas to be with the love of her life and straight up country boy Nik Montgomery. They met while she was in Texas for work and she hit him with her car. And I mean *hit* him. He shattered three ribs, needed surgery due to internal bleeding, and had a cast covering his leg up to his hip.

She felt horrible, so she visited him every day in the hospital while she was there. After a week of spending all their time stuck in a hospital room, they parted ways but continued their newfound friendship. That led to a long-distance relationship. After her wedding to Nik at a barn in Upstate New York, Alyssa then moved halfway across the country to live with him, and Knox, Nik's best friend. Knox was sort of a package deal; he was already living in a cottage on Nik's ranch.

Alyssa's relationship was not the ideal meet cute and not what I expected from her, but right here and now, I couldn't be more thrilled she lives in the middle of nowhere Texas. The perfect hideaway.

As kids, we grew up on the Upper East Side and spent summers at our home in the Hamptons. We were not without privilege. When we weren't in our school uniforms, we were in designer clothes. We had a private chef, a nanny, a maid, anything we could have asked for. Or so you would think.

When I declined my offer to Yale and started school at

NYU, my parents were irate. They always made sure we had every materialist thing, but never gave us what we truly needed–which was their love and affection.

I think their hands off parenting led me to choose NYU and get what they would call a "mediocre" job as a head-hunter. I didn't want to do what was expected of me and I finally did something *I* wanted.

I do just fine on my own. I have a trust fund, but I have never spent a dime. It's been my own way of sticking it to my parents. Honestly, though, I'm not even sure they notice it goes untouched. Fresh out of college, I thought that would be the ultimate FU too, but now I know they couldn't care less.

I let out a deep snort at the thought, receiving a weird look from a fellow traveler.

I should've made my first purchase for a first class flight out of there on Daddy's dime. Why I thought they would care if I touched my trust fund or not is beyond me. Maybe some-where deep down, I thought they would see that I wanted a family more than any amount of money. Now, at almost thirty, I can't help but feel sorry for the younger me who only craved a simple hug.

On family day my first semester at NYU, my mother and father actually scolded me for using my new favorite word *fuck* and wearing an NYU hoodie. My mother's exact words were that my attire was *"very unbecoming for a Hamilton"*.

Now I am finally happy with the woman I have become. I can't help but love my expansive knowledge of curse words and throwing on my favorite thirty-five dollar raggedy NYU hoodie over an obnoxiously priced blouse. Sure, I love designer things. I mean, what woman doesn't? But a pair of cutoff shorts and a hoodie sometimes just make more sense. It's all about balance. And of course, comfort.

Since I moved out of my parents' house to go to college, the designer goods have definitely diminished. I can do without, but my mother continues to send luxurious gifts. Not for me, oh no, they are for when I get photographed with my parents on the occasional brunch that I look the part.

I rub my hand over the leather of my Louis Vuitton luggage.

Except you, Louie. You, I cannot do without.

Pulling my luggage through the double doors to the airport pick-up line, I curse myself for the wardrobe choice. I really wish I had chosen the comfort of my leggings and a hoodie right about now. My feet are absolutely killing me. Sneakers would have made more sense. Airports are not made for heels. I can see that now. But this morning when I got ready, I wanted to set the mood for the day. And nothing does that better than a cute outfit paired with your favorite heels.

Chapter Three
Knox

I have been waiting for Haylee for an hour. I know she's Alyssa's sister and, being Nik's best friend, I should really wait, but I'm not sitting in the airport parking lot all day, like everything revolves around her. Alyssa told me about their upbringing; she probably thinks I'm some country bumpkin that has no life of his own. Not that it would be too far off base. I mean, all I had planned for tonight was a date.

God, how my life has changed. I wonder what younger me would think now. I've come a long way from the kid I once was. I think back to my high school days, growing up playing football, parties, and drinking all night. I remember taking a different girl out on a date every weekend in this very truck. I was such a tool. It's incredible, though, how naïve I was. I mean, what teenager isn't, but it's still upsetting to look back on.

Most people can't pinpoint the exact moment when they lose their innocence, but I can. It lives rent-free in my mind.

"There's been an accident."

It was a normal Friday night for my parents when they went out for dinner and a movie in the city.

"I'm sorry, but there was nothing anyone could have done."

Just like that, my parents were taken from me months before my high school graduation. I stopped going to classes, to parties, and on dates. I went from being the outgoing kid with a bright future to the quiet orphan. Everything changed in a blink of an eye. Everything I thought mattered didn't seem to mean much at that point.

"She can get a cab," I huff, starting my truck and looking in my rearview, ready to back out of my spot. My eyes catch a glimpse of the double doors. A man rushes outside and opens the door goofily, smiling ear to ear, as if the president were about to step through. His eyes are fixated on someone. When I follow his eyeline, I see her and I know with certainty it's Haylee Hamilton.

My eyes immediately draw to her heels, which is all the proof I need that it's her. No one in their right mind wears heels to an airport, let alone around here. My eyes trail up her smooth tan legs to her off-white shorts paired with a black flowing top. Now I understand this man's enamored puppy dog reaction. She's gorgeous.

She gives the man a wide grin and steps out of the double doors. I watch her fake smile instantly drop as she turns away from me. A look of concern and sadness now visible on her face. Her posture falls as she closes her eyes and draws in a deep breath.

I throw my truck back in park and step out of the truck. That's when Haylee's eyes connect with mine, and I hold up my hand to signal I'm her ride. Her fake smile returns and she waves, mouthing, I'm sorry. She makes her way toward my beat up truck and I can't help but regret for a split second not taking Alyssa's car.

"You must be Knox. I've heard a lot about you. Sorry for

making you wait." Her hand stretches to shake mine while she closes the distance between us.

"I've heard a lot about you, too," I say, guiding us toward the tailgate of my truck. "You shouldn't do that, though." My voice is irritated and rough. It's not her fault her flight was delayed.

"Excuse me? Do what? Be late?" Her brows furrow in confusion, and I smile at her expression. It's adorable.

"That too, but no. What if I was some predator? You just told me exactly who I was supposed to be. You just made it so simple." Her eyes go wide and she juts out her chin with a questioning grin, realizing I'm right.

"I . . . I . . . uh. But you are Knox, right?"

I laugh as she questions herself. She knows what she did isn't safe by any means and, for whatever reason, a trace of protectiveness courses over me.

I open the tailgate to toss her luggage in the truck and see her studying me while deep in thought. Now I have her worried. Before throwing her bags in, I reach for my back pocket and hand her my wallet to reassure her. Haylee rolls her eyes as she takes the wallet from my hand, flipping it open to my license.

"Knox Hayes, brown eyes, brown hair, 6'3"." She gives a soft hum and her eyes slowly size me up and down as she matches me to my ID. Looking back down, she brushes her delicate finger over the picture of my face, my breath hitching at the act.

She shrugs her shoulders, and what looks like a genuine smile lights up her face. "I guess we're good to go, then." Before she finishes her sentence, she yanks up on her luggage and pops it on her knee, using the motion to toss it into the truck bed.

Holy shit.

Wasn't expecting that from Little Ms. Manicure.

"Can we make one quick stop?" And there it is. This woman really has no respect, does she? Where the hell could she possibly have to go?

I planned my entire day around her last-minute flight in. I even rescheduled my date with Melanie to pick her ass up. That might've been for the best, though. I am beyond exhausted. Two night terrors in one night. Just when I fell back to sleep, I woke up sweating and screaming.

"It will be really quick, I promise," Haylee announces as we pull up to the store a couple hours from home.

Our small-town pharmacy back home will probably not have whatever this woman needs, so I assure her it is best to stop before we get on the highway home.

Once we arrive at the pharmacy, I park the truck, hop out, and make my way to the passenger side. I'm about to open her door, but before I get there, Haylee jumps out of the truck, nearly falling to the ground. Her oversized purse hurls out of the truck to my feet. She has her arms out, and she totters on her heels, trying to regain her balance.

On instinct, my hands reach out. One hand lands on her hip and the other on the small of her back, much lower than I intended. She inhales sharply and her body freezes in my hands.

I drop my hands from her, letting my hands graze her silk top. For a split second, I wonder if her skin feels this soft.

My eyes lock with the browns of her irises that match her long, wavy hair. The way the light reflects off of them reminds me of freshly tapped honey. I lick my lips at the thought. I am taken off guard when I notice something unsettling. The red rims trace her eyes and the puffiness beneath them. She's been crying. Did I make her cry? Was she crying for the fifteen minutes we drove to the pharmacy? Why the fuck is she crying?

I close the truck door and trail behind Haylee into the

pharmacy. "What are you doing?" she asks as her honey-glazed eyes turn from over her shoulder to meet mine.

"I'm coming with you." I'm not familiar enough with the area to feel comfortable with her prancing around in her little white shorts and high heels on her own.

"Stay," she commands with a smile. It comes out politely, but it sounds like she's speaking to me as if I'm a puppy, which I very well may be right now.

This girl's taken me by surprise, but the men in this town have never seen a woman like her and she's out of her freakin' mind if she thinks I'm sitting in the truck.

"Honey, you are sadly mistaken if you think you're walking in there in that little outfit alone. At home, you may leave your man in the car like a sad little puppy, but not me."

Haylee hits me with a side eye that I am not so certain is because I can't stop calling her *honey* or due to the fact that I am still trailing behind her.

"Have it your way," she says nonchalantly, shrugging her shoulders.

I'm flipping through the latest issue of Southern Living in a small section of magazines when Haylee walks to the counter to pay. She definitely turns heads, but I don't even think she realizes the power she has. Not only have men tried to make eyes at her, but even the women look at her with envy. She's angelic. Mesmerizing. She's a spoiled brat who made my day revolve around her. But fuck, she's beautiful. And I can't take my eyes off her.

I meet her at the counter while she pays for whatever she deemed so necessary to stop for.

"Fuckin shit."

Did she just curse? That was unexpectedly cute. Pretty girls like her don't often curse. Especially the southern girls I'm used to. I can't help but stare as she sifts through her enormous bag.

"My wallet must have fallen when I got out of the truck."

I can't help but laugh. "You mean when you fell out."

Haylee ignores my comment and gives me a pleading gaze as her eyelashes flutter. It's then I realize that I will be paying for what I'm sure is a bright pink nail polish because the princess chipped a nail.

On a sigh, I pull my wallet out and hand her my credit card. I glance over to see what exactly it is *I* am paying for. First Response Pregnancy Test. *Holy fucking shit.*

Chapter Four
Haylee

I have never been more mortified, but hey, I told him to wait in the car. I'm actually happy he came in with me. I am a New Yorker, so I've seen my fair share of creeps, but it was nice to not have to feel on guard. Paul would've dropped me off and went into the bar next door.

One guy simply acknowledged me with a tip of his hat and an "afternoon" and I swear I heard Knox growl. My sister needs me, and some man's ego isn't impeding on that.

Leading me to the truck, Knox opens my door and puts out a hand to help me in the lifted truck. I stare down at his hand. Thinking about how he caught me falling earlier. Every touch since Paul has sent me spiraling into a flashback, but when Knox's hands wrapped around me, it didn't send me straight into a panic.

Knox peers at his outstretched hand I'm glaring at and looks back to me. "I've got you. I won't let you fall."

Ha. Yeah, right.

That's not what I'm afraid of buddy.

If he only knew.

I grip my hand in his and use my weight against his to jump inside.

Again, no shiver of fear at his touch. Maybe it's the fact my sister and brother-in-law adore their friend and I take comfort in that. Alyssa is a great judge of character.

Deep in thought, my eyes catch sight of a shiny clasp beneath my feet on the truck floor. "Aha! Gotcha, you little shit," I say, picking up my Hermes wallet.

I might be dressed in designer clothes, freshly manicured, and waxed for god only knows why, but I am in fact a giant heaping mess. What you see on the outside is pretty much the opposite of what's happening internally. One would say I'm a disaster. My sister, on the other hand, likes to tell me I'm just finding my way.

God, she's annoying.

I smirk just thinking of my sister. I can't wait to finally see New York's biggest city slicker living on a ranch.

The sound of country music fills the cab of the truck. Every so often a song comes on and Knox sings along. Looking at him, I wouldn't take him for much of a singer, but he's actually not half bad.

Singing was always something I enjoyed when I was younger. I did three years of chorus and even some musicals for our high school drama class, but never took it much further.

Why do all the things I actually enjoy doing get put on the back burner? I used to run, sing, read, go out with friends, and host parties. I've never gotten to travel other than for work. I've never been camping or swimming in a lake.

If my parents went on a trip, it definitely wasn't camping, and Alyssa and I definitely weren't invited. It was easier to leave us with the nanny than pretend we weren't both accidents. Which both of us knew to be the truth.

I've always been more concerned about pleasing everyone

else around me first and tiptoeing around what Paul may or may not approve of. God forbid if he came home and I wasn't there to wait on him hand and foot.

"Is there a lake in your town?" I ask, thinking maybe I can start a bucket list. Start doing things for myself for once.

"Right outside of town. Fifteen minutes out, I'd say."

I give Knox a nod of my head, still staring out the window. I can already imagine the feel of the sun hitting my skin, the sound of birds and cicadas as I dive into the lake.

"Have you ever traveled anywhere?" I give him another random question in hopes he will be an aspiration to my bucket list. I also wonder if he's seen outside of his little town. I can't picture him anywhere else with his cowboyish motif.

"Iraq and Afghanistan," he pauses, taking in a breath. "I did two tours in the Marines."

Well, I would never have guessed that, but looking at his muscular arms and chest, it makes sense. He fits the bill.

"Are you still active?" I ask, not knowing how to continue this conversation. I was just making conversation, hoping I wasn't the only one in the world without a stamp on their passport.

Being a Marine is tough enough, let alone two tours. I can't imagine what he's seen and what he's had to do.

"No," he faintly replies, his grip tightening on the steering wheel.

Now I'm intrigued. He doesn't seem like he wants to talk much. It's not a taboo topic. It's just that it can go many directions and we did just meet. Hell, I'm nosey.

"Why'd you get out?"

"Chris Mackey, he was nineteen. He was my ride or die over there, like a little brother. He looked up to me and I depended on him," he pauses to clear his voice. "We were doing a patrol one night, and an IED just went off."

His hands grip the steering wheel tighter. He doesn't need

to say any more. The tone of his voice and the expression on his face tells me everything I need to know. Chris didn't make it home, and I can tell a piece of Knox didn't either.

"Knox," I say to gain a bit of his attention that's now fixated on the road and on his friend Chris Mackey. His eyes meet mine, pain searing from them just at the brief glimpse into his time overseas. "Thank you, for the sacrifices you made," I say with a sad smile and giving him an out to the conversation.

With that, Knox turns up the volume on the radio. Lady Gaga's voice fills the truck and soon it mixes with Knox's deep gruff voice.

I pull my journal from my purse. It's the one that once held all of mine and Paul's important dates, contacts, and my few favorite recipes. Somewhere inside is a list of all the plans I once had. Plans for another life. Before I dig into writing out my new bucket list, I take another peek at Knox. I can tell he's stuck in his head at the mention of his friend. He could use a lighter moment after my prying.

Lady Gaga hits her high notes over the stereo, "oh ah ahhh." I turn to Knox with a wide grin and I let go. I sing much louder and much more energetic than Knox's deep, rugged voice as my hands orchestrate the melody.

Singing to a complete stranger isn't too difficult after they just laid their baggage out for you. I'm surprised by my own voice; I've still got it.

Knox shoots me a wide grin and lets out an addictive laugh. "Holy shit, girl, you can sing."

Holy shit, that smile, it's just as sexy as his laugh.

I open my journal and start my list of all the things I plan to do.

For myself.

Haylee's Bucket List!

Sing Karaoke
Swim in a lake
Run a marathon

I smile down at the list before shoving it back in my purse and shifting toward the passenger door to face Knox. I have two more hours and I want to see that smile as many times as possible.

We have been driving for what feels like forever. I'm used to a quick taxi ride, not hours in a truck. I'm excited to see Alyssa, but I'm even more excited to get her to take this pregnancy test. I know after the miscarriage she's nervous to even be pregnant again. Last time she had a positive test, she was ecstatic. Now, I think she's afraid to even be pregnant again after such heartache.

"How much farther?"

"Fifteen minutes, honey."

I glare at him with a, *seriously, buddy?* look. I'm not sure why he's calling me *honey* after having met me a mere two hours ago, but I don't want him knowing that I actually like the nickname or that it stirred butterflies in my stomach.

Paul used to call me *babe,* and it always made me think of the movie *Babe* with the pig. It made my skin crawl. Nothing about Knox is anything like Paul.

Knox's jeans form just right around his muscular thighs. His dark brown hair has that just-fucked look. Stubble surrounds perfectly sultry lips. Veins peek out from his biceps down to his calloused hands that grip the steering wheel. This man is the epitome of sex appeal.

Paul had his charm in the beginning; don't get me wrong. Tall, blonde, blue eyes, and would make me feel like I was the most beautiful woman in any room. He could sweet talk me, or anyone else for that matter, into just about anything. I think back to all the lost promises of him telling me it'll never happen again.

That it was an accident.

That he loved me.

That no one would ever love me like him.

How I would be nothing, no one without him.

As if he somehow produced the air I breathed. I had been scared for my life in the past. I've taken too many hard hits that left me bleeding or unconscious. I'd been gaslighted and manipulated. He once hit me in the stomach, full force with a wooden baseball bat. Hell, he took a staple gun and cracked it into my skull.

But I kept going back.

Paul made me believe that I was too weak, too fragile to be on my own. I was always the one in the wrong. It was always my fault. Until one night everything just clicked for me. All in a matter of seconds. All the sirens and alarms in my head went off louder than a five-alarm fire.

On that night, I realized Paul hitting me was not my fault.

It never was my fault.

It wasn't because I talked back, or forgot his precious scotch, or didn't agonize over making a dessert.

This was his fault.

Paul had crossed a line at work with one of the victims from a case he was working and was put on desk duty until they investigated. I'm not sure of much else other than he said he didn't do whatever it was they were accusing him of. When

I tried to dig for more answers as to what happened, it turned into just another fight.

When Paul had gotten home, he took to a freshly stocked bottle of scotch harder than usual and finished it off. He then asked me to grab another bottle from the liquor cabinet.

Normally, I was prepared. I was aware of the consequences of an alcoholic not having alcohol. It would lead me into a mound of trouble. Instead of passing out drunk, he'd be coherent enough to beat me.

However, on that day, I hadn't stopped at the liquor store. The owner had continued to creep me out more and more every time I stepped foot inside, and I just wasn't up for trekking four blocks to the next store.

I'm not sure what Paul had disliked more: The exhaustion in my tone when I told him he drank the entire brand-new bottle or that I wasn't prepared with an onslaught of scotch.

In a fit of rage, he threw the coffee table up and over, hitting the TV in the process. He then stood and trudged toward me; sheer rage washed across his once golden-boy face.

I thought I knew what was coming, but the reality was far worse than I expected.

He wrapped his hand around my throat and another gripped my crotch through my jeans. His growl in my ear was a whisper, the scent of alcohol startling my senses.

"I give you everything you want. You don't have to lift a finger other than to cook, clean, and fuck me. You're a good-for-nothing lazy bitch."

Cook, clean, and fuck.

That was what I had been there to do. All while working, maintaining my role as one of the top headhunters for a tech company in NYC, keeping in touch with my small social circle when he ever-so-generously allowed, and donating my time to help *his* department running events, which I would've never dared do if it was for myself. In his mind, I should've been home all day, waiting for him to return, with a pot roast in the oven, feather duster in my hand, just soaking for him.

Asshole.

He eventually had let go of my throat, but only to smack me across my face. I dropped to my knees, gasping for air. That was when I heard it, the cocking of his gun.

"You stupid bitch," he had seethed.

Fear laced through my every never with the steel pushed against my forehead. I can vaguely still hear myself chanting his name over and over again through my shaky voice as tears streamed down my face. The cold steel had pressed against my cheek before there was a loud crack to my skull. Then the world had gone black.

This was when I knew that if somehow got out of this alive, I would never let him sweet talk me again.

Chapter Five
Knox

I haven't told anyone about Chris. I'm not sure what made me confess the few details of his death. Not that I said much to Haylee, but that day will forever haunt me. I've spent countless hours replaying how things could have gone differently. He was a young kid, and he looked up to me. I failed him, even though I know there was nothing I could have done. I still feel like it should have been me who died that day.

The fact that Haylee didn't push the conversation any further only made me think she somehow understood. Deep within her brown gaze, there was a flicker that hinted she too had memories she'd like to forget.

I haven't spoken to anyone about my time in the Marines. Most people want to hear the battle stories and ask if I've ever killed anyone. I never answer them. I will never understand how anyone thinks that's ever an appropriate question. Have I watched someone take their last breath? The faint sound of a prayer on their lips? The lips that kissed their wife and their child only how long ago? The answer is yes; I have taken another living, breathing life and have had them taken from me just the same.

I've always been a master at hiding my emotions. I guess that's a benefit to your parents dying at such a young age. It's as though I've built a tolerance for emotional pain. Learning at a young age how to disguise my emotions and putting on a happy face.

Haylee recognized this, probably because she seemed to do it too. Her lively personality made me go from heavy to light. I swear I felt a shed of pain break away just hearing her sing at the top of her lungs. She was beautiful.

The main house sits on two hundred acres of farmland right outside of town. The house was originally built in the 1960s but has since been updated over the years. It's a bright white, with a porch that wraps around its entirety. With Adirondack chairs and planters strategically placed, it feels like home. Alyssa likes to say she kept it rustic, yet modern. Whatever that means.

Wearing her apron, Alyssa runs from the house to the passenger side of my truck, wrapping her arms tightly around Haylee. She made a huge meal for her sister's arrival. It might be possible she thinks it's Thanksgiving. She cooked a whole turkey, two kinds of mashed potatoes, green beans, rolls, and apple pie. Alyssa is over the moon about her sister coming to visit for a few weeks.

Alyssa and Nik remodeled most of the inside of the house a couple years ago. The modern white cabinets are adorned by four big windows looking out to the ranch. The kitchen opens up into the living room, which peeks at the roof and has two couches facing one another. I always found it interesting; I'm used to having the couch facing the television. A big hearth reaches the highest point of the ceiling with a fireplace and the television above the mantle.

For dinner, we sit at the table in the kitchen with a bench on one side and four chairs on the opposite side. I sit next to Haylee, seated on the bench across from Alyssa and Nik. Haylee and Alyssa banter back and forth the entire meal. Even though they haven't seen each other since Alyssa and Nik's wedding, it is like they never skipped a beat. After dinner, we move to the living room to eat dessert. Nik sprawls himself across the couch, somehow managing to eat from his plate sitting on his chest. Haylee takes the spot on the other couch in the middle of me and Alyssa.

We all relax for a bit, watching the game on TV, and by the time Alyssa gets up to wash a few stray dishes, Haylee has fallen asleep, and somehow found herself nuzzled into my side. I had heard her yawning the entire ride from the airport. I'm sure she's exhausted from the trip. Shit, I'm exhausted from the drive alone.

I can't help but keep taking my eyes off the game to look down at her asleep on me. Even this close, there isn't a single flaw. Perfect bowed lips, long, dark eyelashes, and brown hair that cascades over her breasts. I reach my hand over to push a loose strand of hair behind her ear. I just met her, and the act feels far too intimate but I want to run my knuckles over her jawline. I can't remember the last time I've had a woman snuggled into me. I know she didn't fall asleep on me on purpose, but still, there's something that feels so damn right.

Alyssa walks in and shouts, "Family game night!" Her yelling startles Haylee awake. Her entire body jumps at the noise, clutching me in terror. I can feel her heartbeat racing as she grips herself to the side of my chest.

Waking up in pure terror, screaming, in a pile of sweat is all too familiar to me. Seeing one of your closest friends blown into pieces as their body parts rain down on you will do that, but what's Haylee's reason?

Instinctively, I put my arm around her, rubbing my palm up and down her back and whispering softly, "Shh. It's okay. You're safe, honey." I assure her repeatedly as her eyes dart around the room.

Her quick breaths catch and begin to soften, her hands still gripped tightly on my chest and arm.

"You fell asleep. Everything's okay. You're safe." I tell her the words I've needed to be told countless times.

Those brown pensive eyes look up to meet mine. She's still fisting my arm and shirt with a now embarrassed smile. Somehow, she's even closer than she was when she fell asleep.

"I'm sorry, I didn't . . . I didn't mean to . . . thank you," she whispers softly with such hesitation, her heavy breath dusting my neck. She lets out a deep sigh of relief, the same one I've heard more than once throughout the day.

There is just something about her that's pulling me in. The urge to touch her, still fresh in my mind, I ever-so-slowly trace the back of my knuckles over her cheek. "That's alright. I know what it's like." Once the words fall from my mouth, I can see all the questions she wants to ask me at the forefront of her mind. The thing is, if she asked me, I'd tell her. I'd tell her everything.

I spend multiple rounds of Pictionary and Boggle in a blur. I can't stop thinking of all the reasons why Haylee woke up frightened, hands digging into me for protection and pain ridden eyes. Maybe we aren't as different as I thought.

Alyssa begins a game of Would You Rather, no one having much energy to grab another board game. It's really not a game of *rather* than a slew of questions with no winner. Alyssa and Nik are sitting on one couch, and Haylee is next to me with a blanket wrapped around her.

"Would you rather look like a fish or smell like a fish?" Alyssa asks.

We all respond immediately in unison, "Look."

"Would you rather watch the same show the rest of your life or eat the same thing the rest of your life?" Haylee and I both respond *show,* while Nik and Alyssa say *food.* Nik won't admit it, but I know they binge watch *The Kardashians* together and he secretly loves it.

The TV shows I used to watch are too triggering now. This beautiful bitch called PTSD has a way of sneaking up on you. The random gunshot or explosion will startle me. For fuck's sake, even Guy Farrerri set me off once. I'd rather avoid it completely. Books and the daily paper have been a good replacement since my last tour.

"Would you rather die for the one you love or never have loved at all?" Alyssa asks, ruining my train of thought.

My stomach plummets as my mind traces through every what if. Two times in one day. If I could only go back to that day. I wish it could be Chris with his family playing games. He had so much life to live. He had his entire future ahead of him. Here I am with nothing but a house that sits empty cause I'm far too fucked up to ever live there again. No wife or kids, not even a girlfriend. Just a buddy from high school and his wife.

Why did the person who had so much to live for have to die?

If I could take Chris's place, I would in a heartbeat. What kind of fucked up plan does God really have for us? Could my presence here really be more important than someone else's?

Haylee glances at me. Her expression falters as if she knows where my mind just went. Her hand on my wrist and her thumb grazing my skin pulls me back to reality. When did

Haylee start touching me and how the hell did just that simple act pull me out of my internal spiral?

"I want more dip!" Haylee says, disrupting our game and pulling her hand from my wrist. She gives me a delicate wink.

"On it," Alyssa says, already standing and moving toward the kitchen.

Nik stands as well, following behind his wife. "I need more beer!"

Haylee looks over at me, with a knowing smile and a hint of mischief. "I didn't like that question," she says.

"Thank you," I say through a deep breath.

I feel something ice cold slide between my thigh and the couch, making me flinch. "Sorry!" Her face scrunches at the apology. I lift the corner of Haylee's blanket to see her tiny, delicate feet as she begins to pull them back toward her.

"Your feet are ice," I say as I place a hand back on her foot to confirm what I already know.

"Would you tease me if I said I forgot to pack socks?" Goddamn, her little facial expressions are going to be the death of me. Her eyebrows furrowing and the pout of her full bottom lip.

"In all that luggage you're telling me, there is not one pair of socks?"

"Hey now! It could've been worse. I could have forgotten underwear." She nudges my shoulder and I laugh.

Great. I am definitely picturing her underwear.

With my hand still wrapped around her foot, I rub my thumb against the bottom of her sole to warm it while the other stays placed under me. The fact we just met this morning, and I am somehow now rubbing her feet while I picture the type of panties she wears, is beyond me. I mean, if I want to get technical, it does equal to about the same amount of time as two or three dates would.

"So, where is this lake?" Haylee says, looking down at the

blanket as if she can see through to my calloused hand on her smooth, delicate foot.

"You know, I could tell you, but how about I take you there myself?"

Why did I say that? What the fuck did I say that for?

Did I just become the guy at the airport holding the door for her with the shit-eating grin? Honestly, I don't even think I give a shit, because whatever spell she has on me, making me brush her hair from her face, offering to bring her to the lake and rub her feet, well I don't really give a shit.

"Really? You would?" she questions eagerly.

I can't help but laugh at her childlike excitement about going to a lake. "Haylee, I would love to go to the lake with you."

As Alyssa's giggles approach, I make sure Haylee's feet and my hands are covered from the cold and anyone's prying eyes. Nik's voice quickly fills the room. "Would you rather have to never talk again or rub your nipples every time you talk?"

Alyssa leans toward Nik, laughing and saying, "Well, isn't that obvious. You know I love to talk. Not fair, babe."

"Well, I think on that note it's time for bed," Haylee announces mid-yawn, all while rubbing slow circles over her nipples. Everyone bursts out in laughter. My hand rubbing the bottom of her much warmer foot stills. It's nearly impossible to draw my eyes away from her nipples that are slightly hardening under her blouse.

After only one day, I can't help but think about how I was completely wrong about this girl.

Chapter Six
Knox

Why the hell did I offer to bring Haylee to the lake today? This woman is so far out of my league. Last I knew, she was with some douchebag in New York. Even if she wasn't out of my league, she's an unavailable, unattainable city slicker.

Regretting my offer, I tried talking Nik and Alyssa into taking the day off to either join us or bring her themselves. Nik said he didn't trust leaving the workers alone without one of us staying behind. Nik had inherited the cattle ranch we live on when his parents passed away. Usually, if we need to leave, we feel comfortable with Theo, a ranch hand, in charge, but his wife just had their third child, and he has the next few months off. Alyssa said she has a zoom meeting and won't be done in time. Without his wife going, there is no shot at swapping places with Nik.

Haylee just needs somcone to bring her out to the lake. No big deal. I can do that.

Do not catch feelings, Knox. She's unavailable.

I get in my truck and pull down the gravel drive that's a rock throw away to Nik's house to meet Haylee. She makes her way to the passenger side door of the truck, wearing a white bikini and a sheer fabric wrapped around her waist like a skirt.

It's a fuckin' sight.

But, if I know one thing, it's that this girl is in for a rude awakening. I'm not sure what kind of lakes she's been to, but based on her attire, it's nothing compared to where I'm taking her.

Nik and I frequented this spot as kids. We would spend all day fishing and cliff jumping. There's really no good path to the lake besides trails that local fishermen have made over the years.

I make my way ahead of Haylee to help clear a path to mine and Nik's old spot. I keep hearing her mumble curses under her breath. Every time she does, I hold back a smirk. There's something about hearing curses flying from such a tiny, sophisticated woman I find adorable. Are all women like this in New York?

"Shit."

"Fuck."

She's really not cut out for this, though.

"Um, Knox?" I turn around to see she has burdocks stuck all along her skirt, which is caught on a branch. I laugh at the sight.

"Big city girl not cut out for this, eh?" I tease.

"Well, you could've warned me not to wear flip-flops," she huffs, struggling to free herself.

"But where would the fun have been in that?" I question, as I pluck one of the burdocks off her.

"Fine. Here, just take my sarong," Haylee yells at the branch as she unties the knot from her waist.

For such a tiny piece of fabric, it hid so much of her. Her body's impeccable; toned, petite legs and a smooth, tanned stomach. The sexiest pair of back dimples leading to a perfectly shaped ass.

For fuck's sake.

"You're an angry little thing, aren't you?" I say, holding back a laugh. "Alright, you made it farther than I thought you would. Climb on," I say, hunching down to give her a piggyback ride. She scrunches her eyebrows and scowls at me.

"I'm . . . I'm too heavy, it's okay," she shudders.

Heavy? Is this girl out of her mind? My gear almost weighs more than her.

"You do realize I could bench press almost two of you, right?"

She gives me a hesitant laugh, then huffs toward me and wearily climbs onto my back. With her arms and legs wrapped around me, I can't help but take in the curves of her body. The feel of her chest pressed against my back. Her bare thighs in my tight grip. Why'd she think she was too heavy? Realizing how petite she is only has me thinking of how effortlessly I could flip and bend her in all the right positions, but I chase the thought away as the view of the cliff comes into sight.

I forgot just how beautiful it is here. The lake is surrounded completely by a layer of thick trees and rocky cliffs. The water is calm as it laps at the rocky shore. The peace and quiet is relaxing as the breeze rustles through the trees. I haven't been out here in years. I make a mental note to bring Nik out to our fishing spot.

"Well, this is it," I say, sliding her down onto solid ground.

"What?!" she yells in shock. "How am I supposed to get into the water?"

I didn't think this through. On our hike here, it split off

into where you can fish and where we swim. By swimming, I mean cliff jumping first, swimming second.

It honestly didn't even cross my mind.

Fuck, this girl would never jump this, as much as she might be a pint size trucker.

"You jump," I admit.

Her gaze shifts between me and over the ledge. "Is it dangerous?"

"It's not *safe*, if that's what you're asking, but I know this spot. There are no rocks at the bottom and it's deep enough. You'll be just fine. I've jumped this hundreds of times."

"Are you sure?" she says, looking back at me.

"Look, there is no way I would let you jump if I didn't think you could handle it. If you want, I can go first or we can go back," I offer, giving her an out.

She peers back over the ledge one more time, a smirk slowly transforming into a full ear-to-ear smile. Haylee presses her lips together in thought. "Let's do it."

Haylee is more comfortable with me going first. She says if she hits her head on the way down, at least I would already be at the bottom. Not that it'd happen, but I agree to it.

"You've got this! Now make sure when you jump, you push yourself out away from the cliff!" I yell up to her as I tread water. She closes her eyes and I can see her lips mumbling. I think she's saying a prayer, or cursing.

"Fucking fuck," I hear. Yup. Cursing. I roll my eyes, smiling as I shake my head at her.

"One."

"Two."

"Three."

She screams in excitement on the way down and plummets into the water, belly first. That had to hurt. I am beginning to find Haylee is anything but graceful and that only adds to her charm.

I dive under to grab her and to bring her to the surface. When her head pops up with mine, she's grinning from ear-to-ear, laughing uncontrollably.

She's fine. *Thank god.*

She took that belly flop like a champ.

"Knox! Knox, did you see that? I just jumped off a freakin' cliff!" she laughs, wiping water from her face and running her hands down her wet hair.

I can't help but laugh with her; it's contagious.

"Glad you did it?"

"Yes, that was"—she looks back up to the cliff and to me again—"that was the absolute most freeing thing I have ever done. Possibly the craziest too. You did this as a kid?"

"Yup. My dad would take me fishing right over there," I say, pointing to an alcove in the distance. "He knew I wasn't that into fishing, so every once in a while, we would just end up here."

"Your parents were okay with you cliff jumping as a kid?!"

"Well, I wouldn't say that much. My dad, sure. But my mom. No way in hell."

She lets out a laugh. "Honestly, I can't blame her much. Your parents . . . do they still live around here?" She's all smiles. I hate having to spoil the moment.

"They died in a car crash when I was eighteen." I lean back to float, letting the water take on my weight. I've always found something therapeutic about the water.

"Well, fuck."

I shoot upright, a laugh bubbling from deep inside me.

"'Well, fuck'? That's your response to my parents dying?" I'm still laughing as I speak.

"You didn't let me finish!" she blurts, now mortified, but I still can't help but laugh. "What I was going to say, before you interrupted me, was that it must've been tough to go through at such a young age."

I honestly can't remember the last time I laughed this hard. What a topic of conversation for it to happen. Most people give me the agonizing, *Oh you poor thing* or my most hated, *I'm so sorry* mixed with pity. But not this girl. Not an ounce of pity.

"No, don't be sorry. It's honestly refreshing. Most people just give me a bunch of fake remorse and pity. I can't stand it."

She grins at me, looking less terrified by my admission. "That must've shaped so much of who you are. Is that why you joined the Marines?"

"I guess so, yeah. After their car accident, I didn't have much of a support system. I mean, sure, at first, the entire neighborhood was bringing me casseroles and uncomfortably telling me they were there for me," I admit, taking in her carefully listening, urging me to go on.

I relax my body further into the water before continuing. "But after the dust settled, I didn't have much support, just Nik and his parents. I had a full ride to Ohio State on a football scholarship. But my grades took a dip, and they just didn't want me anymore. Nik's dad was a veteran in the Marines and I loved listening to all his stories. So my dream of college football got replaced by the Marines." I dip my head under the water, trying to cool off but mostly attempting to rinse off my deep dive into the past.

When I come back up from the water, she looks deep in thought.

"So do you regret it?"

Regret not being with my parents in their accident?

Regret not being able to get into Ohio State like my parents and I planned?

Regret going into the Marines?

Regret not being able to save Chris?

"Which part?"

"Not being able to go to college and play football?"

"No, not really. Football wasn't ever anything more than a hobby for me. I mean, I was really fucking good, but it's not like I would've made it to the NFL." Or would've ever wanted to. "The Marines helped me grow up. I needed discipline and structure. Plus, it gave me a chance to get out of a town where everyone looked at me like the orphan kid. Once I got out, I got my Bachelor's in Business with a minor in Accounting."

Haylee throws the stick she's been pushing through a chunk of algae onto the shore. "So, even after being dealt some shitty hands, everything ended up working out for you. Even if it's not exactly how you pictured it."

Definitely several shitty hands. It seems like that's all I get. "I guess I never really looked at it like that. But yeah, I think I'm right where I am meant to be."

Haylee's chin begins to bob in the water. I can tell treading water is tiring her. But some greedy part of me doesn't want this conversation to end. I lace my fingers between hers and quickly tighten the grip and use the force of our intertwined fingers to pull her into me, treading water for the both of us. Her hands wrap around my neck and I study the goosebumps as they trace her arms, wondering if our contact put them there.

"So, what do you do with this fancy business degree, Mr. Hayes?"

Fuck Me.

Mr. Hayes.

The way it rolls off her lips is sexy as hell.

"Well, I help Nik out on the ranch mainly, but I own some properties. Some businesses and homes I rent out."

"It sounds like you did alright by me. I bet your parents would be proud of you." Her approval is oddly satisfying.

I've never been one to care much about what other people think. But her validation means something, along with her recognition of my parents. I'm not sure how she can make any conversation feel so weightless, as if I can tell her my deepest, darkest secrets and I will never get an ounce of judgment.

My thoughts are cut off by Haylee shrieking. She tightens her arms around my neck, holding on for dear life. As if on instinct, my hands grab the back of her thighs as she squeezes her legs around my waist, holding her above the water. I move quickly to the shore, where I can touch the rocky floor of the lake.

Fuck, please don't be a gator.

I probably should've warned her. Standing in the shallow water, with Haylee still wrapped around me, I turn to spot the intruder.

At this angle, I have to look up to meet her eyes. I revel in the sight of us as she gazes down at me. She fits damn near perfect in my arms.

"A turtle? Really?"

"What? I don't see many turtles in Central Park."

With that comment, I toss her back into the lake, her head dipping beneath the water, as I dive in beside her. Thankful for the clear water, I open my eyes to spot her tan, smooth legs and swim my head between them. Standing in the shallow water and lifting her to sit on top of my shoulders, she immediately erupts in laughter. As my hands move to grip her legs, she releases my shoulders, holding her arms out as if she's soaring over the water.

That's when I know catching feelings is inevitable with Haylee Hamilton.

Chapter Seven
Haylee

After getting enough thrill for probably my entire life yesterday, I'm sitting on the back deck reading. It's like a mini slice of heaven out here. Two big Adirondack chairs and a two-person bench are placed around a modern coffee table with a cream, oval rug sprawled beneath it. Fairy lights and lanterns encompass the space, along with fluffy cream pillows and heavy, knitted blankets. I have been sitting here for over an hour watching the sun peek over the tree line of the ranch and workers pulling up to start their daily chores. Every worker has acknowledged me with a wave or a good morning. It's a refreshing change of scenery, from the scowls and shoves on my normal 5 a.m. subway commute. With my coffee and book in hand, I maneuver my blanket around me like a cape and nuzzle into the bench.

This book is captivating, to say the least. The sex scenes are so intricate and detailed. I pause and close the book slightly, my finger holding my place like a bookmark as my head collapses back into the chair. "Holy hell," I sigh in frustration.

For whatever reason, I keep picturing Knox as the main

character. What can I say? He's eye candy. The hard, broad chest and that god forsaken V that dipped below his swim shorts has been engraved in my mind. Then the way he opened up about his parents' deaths broke my heart for the once-teenaged Knox.

I might have had parents that were MIA most of my life, but I cannot fathom how I would feel if I ever lost them. How a boy can endure such pain and come out the other side an ambitious, intelligent, and sympathetic man is intriguing to me. It gives me hope that there is still a chance for me.

"So I see you found my smut," Alyssa says, staring at me and leaning against the entryway.

"Smut?" I question.

"Yeah, smut," she says, pointing to the book. "Romance and drama with a hell of a lot of sex." She smiles proudly at me.

"Lyss!! This is basically porn! It's on your bookshelf in the living room!" I chuckle. "The cover has freakin' daisies all over it!"

"The dirtiest of books do have the cutest covers." She just gives me a shoulder shrug, completely unfazed.

Alyssa sits in the Adirondack chair across from me and places her tea on the coffee table. I admire her, dressed for the day in her work attire. She has always had an effortless beauty about her, never having to wear makeup or fuss with her hair, but always looking so put together.

"So, what do you think of Knox?" Alyssa asks with a grin on her face.

"He's great. I can see why you're all friends," I say, trying to avoid the conversation.

Knox opening up to me about his time in the Marines and his loss as a child had me ready to share details of my life yesterday. At least until that damn turtle showed up. I've never felt so comfortable with someone so quickly. I did explain to him how I went to NYU and into an industry that I thought had purpose, but now I feel like I am making zero impact on the world around me.

I had felt my walls starting to shed the more we talked. There is much more than what meets the eye with Knox.

He consoled me my first day here, practically a stranger, falling asleep on him. Shhh . . . you're safe, honey. Everything is okay. In a complete fog and waking up to a shout, I locked onto him. I knew it was Knox I was latching onto too. It was as if my body knew he would be my protection. His calm, smooth voice instantly put me at ease. How did some part of me just know, within hours, that he would protect me? Something he's proven he'd do on more than just one occasion.

"I saw you fall asleep on him," she says. "I'm not sure why I never put it together until I saw you with Knox, but you two are more alike than you know."

I roll my eyes at her. "Come on, Lyss. We just met. You're not playing matchmaker."

That's the truth. She doesn't need to know I'm picturing him as the main character in this book. We *did* just meet. But for whatever reason, I don't have that instant need to run when he touches me, unlike every other man. Unlike Paul, he actually listened to what I had to say, as if he held onto my every word.

Alyssa raises her hands in defense, laughing as she says, "Not trying to play matchmaker, Hay. But I mean, you guys pretty much already had your first date."

"I asked him how to get to the lake and he said he'd take me. It was really no big deal."

I think back to yesterday at the lake. Him seeing me tire from treading water and pulling me into him to bear the burden. Butterflies had replaced the years of uneasiness in the pit of my stomach as our legs grazed.

Knox was nothing but a gentleman and I feel like an

idiot with a crush. He was just being nice, doing what anyone else would've done. Plus, there is still the whole crazy ex-boyfriend thing I'm not entirely sure I'll ever recover from.

"Whatever you say," she says with a laugh, walking out the deck toward her car. "I'll be back later . . . love you, Hay."

I realize my stomach's growling and I look down at my phone to check the time to see that somehow it's 12 p.m. I read porn the entire morning.

"Ugh." I groan and turn off my phone, walking to the kitchen to make a sandwich. I can't believe Paul is still going at it. When is enough *enough*? What could he possibly think he could say that would make me go back to him. I cringe, thinking of all the times it has worked. I love my new sense of freedom here. I want to feel like my own person again after pretending and being forced into being someone I'm not for so long.

I sit on the bench at the kitchen table, holding my turkey sandwich in one hand and the book in the other.

"Hey there," I hear a familiar greeting and footsteps walk through the door.

It's Knox. I give him a silent wave, too mesmerized by this book. I can't put it down.

Knox's weight shifts next to me on the bench. A heat runs through me at his closeness. I feel him staring at me.

Why is he staring?

Is it the coffee stain on my shirt?

Is he hungry?

Knox walks in and out of this house like he lives here. I'm sure he'd have no problem raiding their fridge. I push the other half of my sandwich toward him, not looking up, because I'm so engrossed in the chapter. He laughs.

"I didn't take you as a girl who reads *that,*" he says, pointing to the cover as I close the book to listen to him.

"It's just a book." I blush knowingly.

Dammit.

Does he know I'm reading porn?

In the kitchen?

"Honey, that is not a book. That's porn," he says, tapping the cover. "Tie me up, call me, Daddy, fuck you so hard you see stars kind of porn."

"No, it's not," I lie, my cheeks beat red.

"Did you get to the part where he instructs her to crawl to him naked?"

Oh my god. I'm mortified. But I guess at least that means he's read it too. Yeah, no, definitely not making it less embarrassing.

"Alyssa left it out one day and I read a chapter, which turned into three. I know what that's about," he says, eyeing the cover with a knowing grin.

"Fine, it's porn," I huff in admission.

He leans in toward me, straddling the bench as he closes the space between us, looking me in the eyes. His fingers brush a strand of hair from my face, causing a tingle to trace down my entire body. I can feel my heart beating and my chest rising and falling with his proximity. Why does he have this effect on me? Maybe it's the spicy book.

Holding my gaze, he leans in toward me, only inches from my lips. *Is he going to kiss me? What the hell?* Then, without hesitation, his head quickly shifts, taking a bite of the other half of my sandwich still in my hand. Turning back to face me, chewing, he gives me a shit-eating grin before getting up from the bench. *Little Shit.*

Knox navigates the kitchen like it's his own, making himself an espresso before walking toward the patio. He turns to me before stepping foot out the door. "And honey, when you get bored with reading it and want the real thing, I live right there." He points out the window toward the adorable cottage.

"I'm pretty sure that's why god made vibrators, Knox." I pull my book up to hide my blushed cheeks.

Holy fuckin' shit. That was the hottest thing I've ever heard out of a man. Once he walks outside, I melt down onto the bench and lay there staring at the ceiling.

With my new pent up sexual frustration, thanks to Alyssa's dirty smut, I decide to make my way into town. It's nothing like back in the city.

The town is small, but filled with so much personality. Two main roads intersect the town, and beyond that, there are dirt roads filled with quaint homes that all look meticulously cared for. The intersecting roads are lined with the town's post office, coffee shop, library, bar, and grocery store. None of the businesses are duplicated. One bar, one barber, one coffee shop, and one grocery store.

I count in my head the number of coffee shops I pass on my commute to work every day in the city. I love how simple it is here; it's refreshing. I mean, who really needs three Star-bucks in a three-mile radius?

The bell overhead announces my arrival as I walk into the coffee shop. I inhale the scent of fresh coffee beans as I take in the room.

Exposed brick covers the wall behind the registers. On it hangs a large black chalkboard, written with all their specialty espressos, macchiatos, and lattes. Leather chairs and couches with strategically placed coffee tables fill the space from the front door to the registers. Another wall is covered entirely in chalkboard paint filled with patrons' names, dates, goofy drawings, and even several faded congratulatory words on their grand opening.

"You must be Alyssa's sister, Haylee," a feminine voice provides, beelining toward me with arms open wide. She's wearing a flowery dress with an apron overtop that sports the same logo on the sign outside.

I accept the stranger's hug, but not without a laugh at the complete 180 I've somehow managed from New York to this small Texas town.

"I am. You're good, how'd you know? I didn't think we looked that much alike, honestly," I question, pulling away from the hug.

"Well, no, I just know everyone in this town, and I heard you were visiting. New face and mention of you coming, I took my chances," she shrugs before tightening the pink scrunchie holding back her long blonde hair. "I'm Annabeth, it's nice to finally meet you."

"It's nice to meet you, Annabeth." I smile wildly and laugh again at the unfamiliar kindness.

New Yorkers do not hug strangers, and they definitely do not have this happy shimmer to them. If the coffee shop doesn't work out for her, she'd definitely make the cut as a princess at Disney World. Her entire personality is infectious.

"So, what can I get you?" she says as she exchanges a coffee for a five-dollar bill for another customer. I can't help but notice she never took an order from them. Does she just remember their order?

"Iced caramel macchiato, please."

"Coming right up," Annabeth chimes, while already making use of the espresso machine. "So, what are your plans while you are here?"

Plans? What are my plans?

Avoid Paul, but I'm certainly not mentioning that to her.

"I'm kind of working on this bucket list I have going on." I smirk, embarrassed, hearing the words as they flow from my mouth.

"That sounds exciting! What is on this list?"

I cannot think of one person I know that wouldn't poke fun at me for having a bucket list, but for some reason I think she genuinely wants to know.

I pull my notebook from my purse, open it to my bucket list, and lay it on the counter. I'm feeling slightly exposed until Annabeth's bright smile lands back on me after reading the page labeled *Haylee's Bucket List.*

"That's a good list you've got there. I bet we could check a few of them off this weekend if you'd be up for it."

I tilt my head toward the side, appraising her honest-to-god genuine smile. It would be nice to make a new friend. Lord knows I need one.

Paul had excuse after excuse why he didn't like my friends. Always coming up with some reason as to why I shouldn't go here or be around so-and-so. It was something I hadn't given much thought to, in all honesty. I thought he had my best interest at heart, but really it was just another way to manipulate me. I bet he would've even come up with some preposterous story about sweet little Annabeth here, too.

"I would actually really like that," I squeak, my voice sounding more cheerful than normal.

After exchanging contact info with my new friend, I walk down main street toward the library, gulping down my caramel macchiato with a grin that I know for certain Annabeth infected me with. To her, it probably seemed like such a small gesture, but to me it meant much more.

The sad thing is that kindness is not something I've ever been used to. She genuinely seemed to care. It's something I haven't had the chance to encounter over the past several years being held captive in my bubble of a life that solely orbited around Paul.

I savor the last few sips of my coffee, hovering near the garbage can, as I take in the library's historical architecture. Intricately designed windows and large white pillars surround the building while dogwood trees blanket the ground with shade from either side.

After weaving up and down stacks upon stacks of books, I finally settle into a comfy leather chair in a common area. Children are working on projects on computers lined against the wall, others focused on textbooks. There is an elderly man reading at a table with who, I assume to be, his wife, knitting in a frenzy.

I feel comfortable; safe even.

It dawns on me that I've felt comfortable here in this small town more often than not. I don't get the usual on-edge feeling where shivers run down my spine or the feeling of my stomach dropping. It's mostly been in the presence of Knox, but here I am blissfully at ease.

Interrupting my train of thought, a young boy no older than seventeen walks past with a struggling look on his face. I make eye contact with him and give him a half smile, as he heads to the librarian a few feet away. On his way back to his computer, he looks even more upset, the rims of his eyes filling with tears. He sits down and places his face in his hands.

I remember feeling so lost at his age, not fitting in with the right crowds, struggling on a test, my middle school boyfriend breaking up with me with a note in my locker saying, *There's other fish in the sea.* I wonder what has him so upset.

I make my way over and kneel down near the computer table, putting my face level with his. He lifts his head toward me as he wipes a few stray tears away.

I pull a small packet of tissues from my purse and slide them onto the desk.

"My name's Haylee. I couldn't help but notice how upset you were walking by me. Are you alright?"

His green eyes meet mine as he collects himself.

"I'm alright. It's . . . it's just this college admission essay. I can't write this. It's bullshit."

I hold back my chuckle at him cursing. "Well, guess what . . . umm . . ."

"Cade."

"Guess what, Cade?"

"What?"

"I happen to be fabulous at writing essays. Do you mind if I take a look?" I say, taking the seat at the computer beside him.

"You can, but it's pretty pointless, anyway."

"Why do you say that?"

"Well, it's kind of ironic, but the essay is to write about a time you overcame a challenge or setback. I planned out for days what I thought I was going to write, but now it's more of an angry letter to myself of how I saved up all summer to only end up being short fifty dollars for the application fee." His voice cracks, getting out the words.

This is one thing I am truly grateful my parents gave me.

Never having to worry if there was food on the table, a roof over my head, or a college application fee to afford.

Cade should be worried about if the printer has enough ink for his essay, if the girl at study hall has a crush on him, or if he's going to wear a funky colored tux to prom.

"I see . . . well, let's just say you stumbled over the extra fifty dollars right here in the library. What would you write your essay about?"

Cade goes on to explain his mother's battle with cancer. He tells me how she is unable to do all the things she once did for her family. Telling me how his father works two jobs to make up for her loss of income. How they barely see him anymore unless it is to take his mom to treatments.

Cade took on all the roles his mother couldn't tend to and all the ones his father didn't have time to. He makes breakfast for his little sister and packs her lunches, cleans the house, mows the lawn, and even does the grocery shopping.

My heart breaks at his story. The harsh realities of adulthood crashed down on him at such a young age. Making me think of Knox and all the things he probably had to take on after his parents' deaths.

As it turns out, Cade's mother is now in remission, and even though she's the one that battled cancer, he overcame it too.

We decide it's best to work on the application one step at a time. Money being last.

I sit back and read at the desk next to him as he types out his essay that he had written out in his notebook. I help him with the occasional spelling and grammar errors, and serve as a sounding board for him to bounce ideas off of.

Coming time for the payment portion of the application, he sighs heavily. "My mom still isn't well enough to go back to work and I know my dad would pay for it, but it just feels wrong asking."

"Cade, you're doing so much with your family and your schooling. You shouldn't have to worry about this, too."

I dig into my purse and take out my wallet. I cannot let him walk away from applying to a college after all that he's been through. I pull out my wallet and flip through, pulling out my debit card. I hesitate, a light bulb flickering in me.

This is what I want to use my trust fund for; making sure kids who don't have the means to afford things like college application fees can do so. I am sure there is so much more they'd need help with down the line, too. My trust won't be able to help every student, but I'm sure I can figure out a way to raise more money to help more and more kids.

Cade's not the first and certainly not the last. I slide my usual card back into my wallet and I pull out the debit card linked with my never-touched trust fund and slide it across the table toward him.

His eyes well up again with tears and he jumps into me, wrapping his arms around my neck.

"Thank you, Ms. Haylee."

"Of course, buddy. Meet back up here tomorrow. We have to apply to some back up colleges too. Just in case."

Chapter Eight

Knox

"Dessert?" I ask Melanie from across the table.

"I think you know what I want for dessert," she responds cooly.

How tacky.

I had the biggest crush on this girl all through high school. It only took me until thirty-two to actually get a date with her. She's beautiful and curvy in all the right places. Without fail, every time I'm in the bank and she's counting my deposit, I wonder what it would feel like to grab onto her ass as she rides my dick.

Right now, though, I'm looking at her, watching her mouth move, and I can only think of Haylee's honey-soaked eyes.

My attention sips further. It's Haylee, Alyssa's entitled, stuck up sister. What do I care?

Except she's not anything I thought she was. She's easy-going, caring, and hands down the most stunning woman I have ever laid eyes on.

Then add in that I can see something else deep within her,

the demons she carries. She hides it well, but as someone who also carries their own demons, I know there's so much more to her than what meets the eye.

I doubt Haylee would imply she wants to fuck me in lieu of dessert on the first date.

Focus, damnit. Melanie, you want Melanie.

I'm finally out with her and she's ready to go. I shouldn't be thinking of Haylee. I should care about what Melanie's eyes look like, gazing up at me while she's on her knees with her lips around my dick. Something I have craved for years.

Haylee's eyes flash up at me with her pink polished fingers wrapped around my length.

I feel myself tighten through my jeans.

What is wrong with me?

What kind of guy thinks of another girl's mouth on his dick on a date?

It was that damn vibrator comment. I took my break to squeeze in a nap on the deck and instead of being able to get some shut-eye, I ended up running into Haylee in the kitchen and thinking of Haylee with a pretty pink vibrator.

I need to get the fuck out of here.

"Check please."

Last night was the first night this week I didn't wake up screaming Chris's name or in a puddle of my sweat.

I slept like a goddamn baby.

No thanks to Melanie, even though I'm sure the sex would've been great, but she's just like every other date I've been on. She put on a show and tried to say what she thinks I want to hear instead of just being herself.

I had been excited about the date with her, too. I'm not

saying Melanie isn't attractive or charming, she is just very cookie cutter. Nothing about her captivated me.

Sure, I could've had some fun with her, but when it comes down to it, it's easier to take care of the deed myself, rather than deal with obsessive texts and calls that usually follow a one-night stand. I'd rather find someone I can really see myself with down the line, but every woman I seem to meet is lacking any sort of emotional connection.

There's been a handful of women who've made it clear they want to stay home to cook, clean, and be barefoot and pregnant. Which is fine, however, I just don't think a woman like that is right for me.

I need spontaneity and charisma in my life. Someone who's going to challenge me, keep me on my toes, make me laugh, and be able to be there when I'm not at my best. Someone who is driven and doesn't want their sole purpose in life to revolve around caring for me.

So, after walking Melanie to her car and saying goodnight, I went back to my cottage, took a nice long shower, and thought of those big brown eyes with my hand tight around my dick.

I may have gotten my first good night's sleep in months. But that's not to say I didn't feel like a complete asshole jerking off to a possibly pregnant woman in a committed relationship.

Chapter Nine
Haylee

I'm hiding out in the bathroom, waiting for Alyssa. Last night, she decided she was ready to take a pregnancy test. She told me to meet here at 6 a.m. Something about the first pee of the day being potent, but I'm too excited sitting here. I pull out my phone to check the time, unsuccessfully trying to ignore the multiple notifications on my screen.

Today 2:06 AM

PAUL

Everyone saw me open your little package

You have some fuckin nerve

I'm done playing this game. Get your ass back to the city

"Instant coffee, instant rice, instant breakfast. So, tell me whyyy they have not made an instant pregnancy test?!" Okay, so, Alyssa is a little impatient, but I mean, it's three minutes.

She's the one who kept not wanting to take the test. Now the girl's got to wait.

"Distract me, Hay."

I let out a loud sigh. Now's a better time than any to lay it all out. She's one of the few people that knows the truth about mine and Paul's relationship.

"So, you know how we were confused about why Paul broke in and ransacked my apartment? Well, I finally figured out what he was looking for. I was in the closet packing before coming here and I had opened a drawer and heard a clunk. Like something fell. I didn't think twice about it because I just wanted to get out of there. So, I'm looking at my cowgirl boots from your wedding, debating if I should bring them . . . you know, the ones everyone wore with their bridesmaid's dress? I was happy to have a reason to wear them again, so I shoved my foot in, and there it was. A fucking engagement ring box, Lyss."

Her eyes are glued to me. I definitely distracted her.

She looks at me like there's more to the story. "You have been waiting for a ring for years. What an ass! So then what?"

So then what? As if I ran back into his arms or something. Sure, I wanted a proposal and wedding at one point, but I haven't thought about it in a very long time.

"So, I mailed it to the police station in a box that said Attention: Paul Phillips."

She gives me a face of horror before erupting into laughter. "Holy shit, you're a badass!"

I'm not sure if hiding bruises covering your entire body or sleeping in the tub because your inebriated boyfriend is just sober enough to still expect you to put out is exactly "badass." But I did feel pretty badass mailing that box. This was absolutely the *fuck you* I needed.

I am nervous, though, that I poked an already angry bear . . . one that by day is apologetic and then a couple hours into happy hour is seething anger. Unfortunately, I can't help but read through the unanswered texts.

The egg timer in the shape of a chicken blares, interrupting my thoughts. Alyssa decides I will be the one to read the results of the little plastic pee-covered stick. Alyssa's sitting on the closed toilet bowl lid, her head slumped between her knees. I know how badly she wants to be pregnant again, but she's also terrified to be pregnant after having miscarried.

I lift the hand towel that covers the test sitting on the vanity, seeing the large pink plus sign staring back at me. My sister's eyes meet mine from behind me in the vanity mirror. Without having to say a word, Alyssa already knows from my expression through the mirror that it's positive.

Alyssa cries tears of joy, which soon turn into tears of fear and sadness. I wrap her in my arms, holding her, knowing there's not much else I can offer. She's been through months upon months of trying to get pregnant, the hundreds of ovulation tests, pregnancy tests, and a missed period that turned into a positive pregnancy test.

She's done this. She's done all of it. Only to not ever be able to hold her sweet angel in her arms. I cannot begin to fathom the pain she has felt . . . how it can all end in an instant. I know that fear will eat at her every day until the moment she can hold this baby in her arms. Unlike before, I'm not comforting my sister through a phone call—I'm here right beside her.

After a few moments of composing herself, Alyssa brushes away her tears, gathering her courage, and heads out the door to work.

A while later, I'm sitting in my chair on the porch, catching up on work, when my phone lights up with a text from Paul. Before opening it, I text my sister first.

HAYLEE

I'm so freakin' proud of you.

ALYSSA

I'm a nervous wreck.

I'm not telling Nik until we go away. I want it special for him.

HAYLEE

I'm here for you

I love you

ALYSSA

Love you

Hay?

HAYLEE

Yea?

ALYSSA

I'm proud of you too.

Today 7:02 AM

PAUL

Baby let's talk

It will never happen again. I fuckin promise you

Come back, put on my ring and we can plan the wedding you always wanted

Where are you I'll come get you

Chapter Ten
Knox

I tried avoiding the main house this morning. I feel like a loser for having thought of Haylee the way I did. Who thinks of another man's pregnant woman like that? There's just something about her that pulls me in.

But my need for a decent espresso outweighs the fact I think I'm a tool right now. Nik hates coffee, so he doesn't understand. But ever since Alyssa introduced me to espresso, I've been coming over every morning to use her fancy Williams Sonoma espresso machine.

It's how we bonded, and now she is one of my favorite people. She is exactly who I want in Nik's corner, too.

I grunt in frustration.

I wish I had just bought the damn machine when Alyssa had sent me the link. It would be worth the two thousand dollars right now. I just never saw the point. My morning walk here and espresso on the porch has become a morning ritual.

So, here I am tiptoeing across the wide planked floor, afraid to wake anyone. I need to get in and out. And quick. I'm trying to find a travel mug in the cabinet because today, I have no intention of sticking around. Not immediately seeing to-go cups, I mentally curse out Alyssa for being one of those psychotic people who use a glass coffee mug in the car. I mean, really? Who does that?

Quietly, I juggle multiple mugs in one hand while maneuvering others to another side of the cabinet. That's when I spot the small jar labeled *Prenatal Vitamins*. I feel my chest ache with disappointment.

Well, I guess that answers that. *I'm really going to hell now, aren't I?* I let out a heavy sigh and tilt my head to the ceiling.

"Sit." I hear Haylee's soft, demanding words. She places her hand on my elbow as she takes one of the several cups I'm awkwardly holding from my hand and they clank together as she places them back into the cabinet. You would think the confirmation of her being pregnant would obliterate my physical reaction to her, but it does absolutely nothing. The goosebumps run down my spine all the same.

Stretching around me to put the mug away, I glance down. Her pink silk bathrobe barely covers her skin-tight white crop top and blue pajama shorts.

A smart man would be heading for the door, but I am, in fact, not a smart man.

I lean against the counter to admire her while she organizes the mess of mugs.

Her breasts are a perfect handful, with perky nipples poking through her tank top from the cool morning air. Fuck. I have never been so grateful for a cool morning. The muscles of her exposed stomach flex as she reaches to return another mug.

My mind floods with images of my tongue tracing the ridges from her stomach up to her perfect tits.

I know I've seen her in a bikini, but for whatever reason, even wearing more clothing, this feels much more intimate.

When I meet her eyes, she gives me a knowing smile,

having obviously caught me in my perusal. Haylee places the last mug back into the cabinet before reaching out her hand to mine. I can't help but notice how dainty her hand is in mine as she pulls me to the chair at the kitchen table.

"Sit, I got this. You were nice enough to pick me up from the airport and take me to the lake. The least I can do is make you a coffee."

I came to the thought of her sucking my dick last night. She owes me nothing, but I follow her instructions, nonetheless.

I sit, leaning back in my chair to enjoy the view. "Espresso, actually," I correct with a grin. She smiles and floats around the kitchen.

I'm not sure why she has the effect she does on me. She's not my type. Big city, fancy clothes, handed life on a silver platter. Yet I feel this undeniable connection to her.

You cannot fall for her, asshole. She's pregnant. She's with someone else.

I watch her as I silently try to list all the reasons in my head. I cannot let her have this effect on me, but I'm too entranced by her. She has a bright smile on her face and I take pride in knowing that it's a genuine smile, not the one I have seen her turn on and off.

Sunlight pours into the kitchen and she stops to admire it, looking out the floor to ceiling window. She looks fucking angelic as the sun illuminates her. Haylee lets out a big deep breath and her entire body relaxes, as if the warmth from the sun released all the tension in her body. Little does she know, I have the better view.

"So, what has you up so early?" she asks, placing her perfectly made espresso in front of me before heading back toward the sink.

"I'm heading into town for a bit. I like to get in and out

before the farmers market today." Her face lights up like she just saw John fucking Mayer.

Why'd I say farmers market? I'm in for it now. There will certainly be no avoiding today.

"A farmers market?!" she squeaks, turning her head to look at me as she cleans a dish in the sink.

I let out a knowing sigh. Aware of the fact that I am her little puppy at her feet and if she says roll over, I will. I beat her to the punch, taking down the rest of my espresso in one shot before standing. "Be in my truck in ten."

Her smile lifts as I make my way toward her. My front inches from her back, I can't resist the urge to skim my knuckles down the silk of her bathrobe as I speak. "Thank you for the espresso, Haylee," I mumble, my words sounding deeper than normal. My knuckles continue to travel to her elbow, where the sleeve of her robe ends. My palm runs down the length of her arm to meet her soap covered hand.

Her breath hitches as my calloused hand engulfs her delicate one. She relaxes as I caress my thumb back and forth in the palm of her hand. I take in the feel of the water and her soft skin gliding against mine.

As I lean closer to whisper in her ear, the soft silk of her robe brushes against me. "Honey, just know, as much as I enjoyed watching you prance around in the kitchen, wearing next to nothing, don't you *ever* think I expect anything in return."

Haylee's phone won't stop going off. It's every few minutes. Every time it dings with a text, she doesn't read it. Every time a call comes in, she quickly declines, not even glancing down.

Out of the corner of my eye, I see her finger on the window, tracing the outline of the mountains as we drive into town. She's wearing converse, distressed denim shorts, and the same white cropped tank I saw the outline of her nipples in less than thirty minutes ago. Except now she's wearing a bra underneath with a white shirt unbuttoned overtop. I smile, knowing I got the better view of her in that shirt.

The sound of her phone echoes through the truck again, her finger immediately declining the call. Maybe she thinks it's rude to answer in the car.

"So, what made you decide at the last minute to come to Texas? This is your first time, right?" Her phone rings once more and with another quick press, she declines it.

"Umm," she hesitates quickly before continuing, "My apartment got broken into. I felt it was as good a time as any."

My hand grips the steering wheel tighter. My knuckles turn white knowing someone had the ability to break into her apartment. The one place she should feel the safest. Maybe that's why she's so on edge.

"What did the police say?" She quickly declines a call again before her phone even chimes again.

"Don't know," she says with a smile and a shoulder shrug. "Never called them."

Has this girl lost her mind? She is being too casual about this. Has New York's crime rate gotten that bad where they just ignore someone breaking into someone's home?

Ding.

"Why the hell not?"

Ding.

Ding.

Shit, that's getting annoying. I glance down at her phone in her hand, not giving a fuck if I'm being nosey.

I recognize the name and a sense of jealousy immediately courses through my veins.

"You can answer that you know, I don't mind," I say, pointing toward her cell phone.

She shoots a quick look at me in embarrassment. She walked into a pharmacy in the middle of nowhere with a complete stranger to have them buy her a pregnancy test and walked out with a smile. She rubbed her nipples in front of a complete stranger. She read smut at the kitchen table. She doesn't get embarrassed, but I keep seeing tidbits of this unrecognizable timid side of her.

"Sorry. It's okay, not important," she assured, silencing the phone and putting it in the tiny bag she has today. *How many bags did she bring for a few weeks on a ranch?*

"Seriously, if you have to take it it's fine. It seems important."

Her eyes shoot back to me as if she's questioning her next words. She lets out a deep breath. "Paul hasn't taken the breakup well, and this has been my new normal for a while now."

Breakup? I really need to listen better to Alyssa when she's babbling. The woman can talk. I like it quiet in the morning and she talks really fast.

"I'm sorry, I didn't know. How long ago did you two break it off?" My eyes come off the road to meet hers. She looks pained again, like she might cry. I'm sure being hounded by your ex is infuriating, but this seems borderline harassment.

"Two months ago. It's been like this ever since," Haylee answers.

Two months?

Two months and this is her normal.

This *is* harassment.

If he has no issue harassing her, I wouldn't be surprised if he was the one responsible for breaking into her apartment. Fucking prick.

Haylee's chin quivers and her eyes well with tears. I slow down and pull off to the shoulder of the road. She glances at me, confused, then gives me a smile in an attempt to mask the pain. Like hell if she thinks I'm going to just continue to drive and ignore her crying right beside me.

I can see the pain in those deep brown eyes, but now I know what I couldn't quite put my finger on all this time. It's fear.

I want to take it all away, take every ounce of pain and make it my own. I turn my body toward her, my eyes searching hers as she holds back tears. "Haylee, did he break into your apartment?"

I want her to tell me, to let me hold on to some of this pain for her. I'd carry it all just so she didn't have to.

Her lips curled together in a line and she shakes her head vigorously, like if she speaks, the tears will break free.

I reach my hand on hers and squeeze it tight. "You're here with me now. I won't let anything happen to you."

"But it already did." Her words are a whisper as she finally lets her tears spill.

What happened to her?

What did he say to her?

Did he hurt her?

My mind races through the endless possibilities. Fuck. How could someone cause so much pain to the person they're supposed to love and protect, all while carrying his child? I already know I'd do everything possible to protect Haylee, and I only just met her.

I place my hand on the side of her head, cupping her ear, swiping my thumb to wipe her tears. Her head tilts, relaxing into my palm, as if my touch somehow alleviates some of that pain. The same as when she saw the sunrise.

"What happened, Haylee?" Her eyes graze down to my hand, holding tightly to hers. I'm unsure as to when I grabbed it, but it all feels so natural.

"He isn't a good man. He was. At first. Then he started drinking more." She takes a deep breath and turns to look out the window before she continues. "Then he started hurting me, and I . . . I kept going back to him."

My stomach somersaults as images of her hurt fill my mind. "It started out as a slap or a punch, but as time went on, it only kept getting worse. A broken arm, fractured ribs, stitches." She pauses and turns back to look me in the eyes. "The last time he . . . he held a gun to my head," she confesses as more tears streak her face.

I will kill this fucking scumbag. I hide the rage that simmers through my veins. She's seen enough anger; she doesn't have to bear witness to my own.

This woman is so goddamn strong. If she ever questions herself because of this piece of shit, I will have no problem putting her mind at ease each and every time.

I unbuckle Haylee and pull her onto my lap. I hug her tightly, placing my hand in her hair as I guide her head to my shoulder. My arms encase her and I trace my hand up and down her spine. Her cries become silent, but I know she's still crying as her body trembles against me. I've heard similar cries and I tuck the memory quickly away.

Turning my head to her ear, I whisper, "I won't let anyone hurt you again. I've got you. You're safe, Haylee."

Her head tilts into the arch of my neck, her breaths

brushing along my skin. Softly, she places a kiss on my pulse. And goddamn, if I don't fall for her right then and there.

Chapter Eleven
Haylee

It's been two months since I broke it off with Paul. I am a single twenty-eight-year-old. I am allowed to gawk at men. Well, not men plural. Really just one very rugged man, a very caring man, whose presence consumes me and provides comfort I've longed for.

Even in the beginning with Paul, I never felt this. My stomach flutters at the thought of Knox. A vibration pulses inside me when he's near. The way his eyes cut through me, no one has ever looked at me with such intensity. Then there's his touch; god, his touch completely blinds me. When he held me against his chest and I sobbed into his shirt, I felt safer than I have in so damn long.

I study Knox speaking with one of the vendors. Can guys have resting bitch faces? Cause if so, Knox has it down pat. Maybe resting asshole face?

His jaw is chiseled. His lips are drawn straight, hidden behind dark stubble. His brows are furrowed with a wrinkle between them from too much sun. But I know Knox, behind the rough exterior, is a gentle and compassionate man. He's let me tug him around the farmers market, going from booth to booth, after having held me while I cried.

I continue to look him up and down. I've been through enough bullshit. If I want to gawk at a man, I'm sure as hell going to.

Maybe it's the cowboy hat?

My eyes graze the tight white t-shirt, accentuating the muscles from his neck down to his chest. *Oh god.* His blue jeans fit his ass just right, and his belt sports an oval buckle that his shirt so perfectly tucks behind. I try to make out the engraving on the buckle.

Holy hell.

Forget the buckle. I can see the entire length of him outlined through his jeans with the way he's standing. *Wow.* I fan myself with a pamphlet about the benefits of raw milk.

Knox shakes hands with the gentleman and strides toward me. *Shit.* I hope he didn't see me staring at his junk. My eyes land on his dick again.

What the hell is wrong with me?

I look up with a doofy smile on my face like I'm seven and caught with my hand in the cookie jar. Good lord, do I want the cookie.

Okay, get your shit together. You've seen a man's penis before. And this one's even tightly tucked away.

I run my hand through my hair and straighten my smile, making eye contact this time.

Just don't look at his dick.

Don't look at his dick.

Don't look at his dick.

I look.

And this man does what?

"Like what you see, honey?" Oh, he definitely knows.

"I was trying to make out what's on your buckle. What is that?" I say, pointing down to his buckle.

Great, now I'm pointing at his dick.

I've officially made it worse and I feel the blush spread from my cheeks to my chest.

"If you ask nicely, I'll be happy to show you." He winks. Of course he winks, as if he knows that is the key to my undoing. I need to stop reading that damn book. It makes my brain think ungodly things.

Knox mentioned he also came to town to run into the post office to mail out a package. So, I told him I'd wait in the coffee shop, not wanting to continue to intrude on his plans. I am happy to wait, especially after he allowed me to go to the farmers market. He encouraged me to take my time and even pointed out little trinkets that caught his eye and told me stories about the families at each booth.

I got sunflowers, the reddest strawberries I've ever seen, and a lotion made from goat's milk. These people are really into their milk. I did see a beautiful gold ring with multiple diamonds in a crescent. The diamonds were fanned out unevenly to look just like rays from the sun. I pulled it on and off my finger, debating if I could justify the purchase. The ring reminded me of the peace I felt as all the tension fell away watching the sunrise this morning.

I've never been able to appreciate one like I did today. Living in New York, it's rare to have an unobstructed view. When I saw it, it brought me peace and an overwhelming sense that everything was going to turn out okay for me. I didn't buy the ring; it wasn't a necessity for someone who's paying rent on one income. Knox had given me a sad smirk, as if he knew what the ring signified: The overwhelming sense of tranquility and agony of being set free. Even if it was for only a moment.

My first cup of coffee is for the well-being of others, but my second is all for me. I cherish every drop while I listen to Annabeth gush over one of the vendors she had just met.

"Oh my word, he was as fine as my momma's china," she admitted, blowing out a deep breath.

I cannot help but laugh and be entranced by her story of how they met. As much as we are two very different people, I can really see myself being friends with Annabeth. She is a breath of fresh air. She would never survive the city, and for that reason alone, I adore her.

"So, are we still on for this weekend? I have the whole thing planned."

I glance past Annabeth, noticing Knox leaning against the truck, one boot behind him, pressed into the passenger side door.

"Yes, definitely," I say, standing, grabbing my coffee and purchases from the farmers market. "Just text me the time and place. I've got to run though, my ride's here," I say, leaning in to give her a hug.

When did I become a hugger?

Walking out of the coffee shop, I realize Knox is standing there, not to get my attention to leave, but to open my door. What a gentleman. Over the past five years, I cannot think of one time Paul ever opened my car door, or any door for that matter.

I fail trying to rearrange my armful of goodies, and the coffee makes it impossible to have at least one free hand. Knox must notice because I let out a gasp when he all but scoops me up by the hips and places me on the passenger seat.

Goddamn.

That was sexy. He didn't even struggle, just picked me up and placed me how he pleased. My knees are pointing out toward the open door of the truck, but Knox doesn't back away. He's still facing me as his hips press against the inside of my open thighs.

This man's going to be the death of me.

"I got you something," he says, handing a bag to me.

What could he have possibly gotten me? I reach in, pulling out a rectangular box. In my hand is the newest iPhone. I look up, my eyes searching his in confusion. This is too much. This is a one thousand dollar phone. Is he mental?

"What is this?" My voice is more stern than normal. "This is too much, way too much," I insist. "You can't just give someone a brand new iPhone, Knox."

"I am pretty sure I can and I just did, Haylee."

"I can just change my number. It's really not a big deal. It's just a few phone calls," I murmur, even though blocking his number and changing my number has already proved to be ineffective. Being a police officer gives Paul the advantage.

"And have you?" he asks.

My eyes look down at the phone while my face tells him all he needs to know.

"It's yours, honey. I wouldn't give you this if I didn't want to. You have a new number and he cannot trace it back to you. I put my number in your contacts. If you *ever* have an emergency, I want you to know you can always call me," he says in all seriousness. "Even if it's 3 a.m. and your book just isn't cutting it," he says, lightening the mood.

I run my hand down his arm until it grazes over his hand placed on the passenger seat. As if on instinct, Knox's fingers intertwine with mine. His thumb traces patterns across the back of my hand. Our eyes sear into one another's, and I study the sincerity and protectiveness in his expression.

I lean in and give him a kiss to the cheek. "Thank you," I whisper.

Deciding I will keep the new phone, I hop down out of

the truck. Knox moves aside as I run across the street, smiling with my old phone in hand. I hold it high over the garbage can and lock eyes with Knox. When the hundreds of texts, voice-mails, and pictures of unwanted memories land with a thud in the garbage, another weight lifts from my shoulders.

Across the street, Knox is laughing. I run back to his outstretched hand, grinning ear-to-ear, giggling. When I reach him, I use his hand as leverage to help me jump into the seat of his truck. And this time, I do it like a pro.

Chapter Twelve
Haylee

It's been over a week that I've been in Canyon Falls. I came here with zero intentions, but with every day that passes, I think about how happy I am here. Sure, it could be the fact that being hundreds of miles from Paul eases my anxiety just a fraction. Or the fact that my sister and brother-in-law have made me feel nothing but at home. I think I'm actually starting to think this small town is my happy place.

The fresh air, miles of open land, and the way the stars light up the sky at night all make me feel at peace. The late nights with Alyssa, Nik, and Knox, talking and playing games, gives me a new sense of belonging. People on the street remember me by name and when Annabeth asks if I want my usual, it makes me feel right at home. How in such a short time do I already have a freakin' usual?

Alyssa took me one night to watch Nik and Knox play on something they call *Beer League*. At first, I wasn't sure what a beer league was. I had envisioned a bunch of grown men sitting around competing to see who can chug the fastest. Like some sort of food eating competition, but with beer. I now know that it's actually a men's baseball league for the town, but after watching, I don't think I was too far off.

I know it's not much, but I feel like I'm a part of something. A part of this small community that welcomed me with open arms. My life has done a complete 180. In the city, I've gone to the same coffee shop for six years and they still don't know my name, let alone my order. I don't miss the constant "watch it lady" comments that come with the ongoing dead arms walking down the packed city streets, or the strangers jumping in your cab just as you're about to slide in.

Here in Texas, people act as if they have all the time in the world. Complete strangers will stop to tell you directions. When someone greets you with a *Hello, how are you?*, they actually expect a response to the question and genuinely care to hear it.

Coming here, I now feel like my life has always been in a constant state of chaos, but now, especially in this moment, curled up beside Alyssa as she researches all the foods not recommended to eat while pregnant, I feel anything but chaos.

"Blue Cheese! Really, kid?" she says, looking down at her stomach.

I can't help but laugh. She's been playing cool, calm, and collected, but I know deep down she's a nervous wreck. Her first pregnancy, she told Nik by having him open a box. Inside was a onesie made into a jersey with their last name printed on the back. Alyssa's further along than she was the first time she announced the pregnancy to Nik. She is unsure about telling him the same sentimental way because it lost its allure. Even knowing how drastically the chances of a miscarriage drop with each and every week, she is still afraid it can all end in tears.

I never could grasp the idea of why it's society's "norm" to not announce a pregnancy until you're past the first trimester. If it were me, I would want my closest of friends to know in case I need them to help guide me through the unbearable pain. However, I guess, on the other hand, I couldn't imagine having to explain more than once how you're no longer expecting a child.

I get that Nik struggled, but if I know Nik, he would want to know, which is why I have been encouraging her to tell him since the day she took the test. He would want to be there to help drown out all her fears and reassure her. My biggest fear is her never telling him at all. That history repeats itself, and my sister has to go through it again without her husband. Even though I came here under shitty circumstances, I am glad to be here, supporting her in any way I can.

Alyssa gasps as her eyes go wide in shock.

"What? Another cheese you can't eat?" I say in a laugh, rolling toward her on the bed to look at whatever she sees on her phone.

Alyssa points her phone screen toward me. The sight of his name makes my stomach drop and the familiar invisible hold clenches around my throat.

PAUL

Where the fuck is she Alyssa?

By this point, he knows I disconnected my phone. I'm certain he can't connect me to the new number on Knox's plan. The fact he's texting Alyssa, though, means he knows I must be here.

It was only a matter of time.

He's been to my office, and my few usual spots in the city asking questions. My boss Eileen had warned me as much when I called her to let her know that after my week's vacation was up, I will be working remotely from Alyssa's house.

The office was never a place I had to be at in person, but it was a safe haven for me at one time. Looking at it now, Paul was never too threatened by Eileen, maybe because people don't see a sixty-five-year-old, gray-haired woman as much of a threat.Eileen was aware of what went on at home. She never flat out told me, but I would put money on it that Eileen had once walked in my shoes.

"Is he freakin' serious? What does he even want?" Alyssa huffs as her fingers frantically pound out a response. She turns the phone back to me once she's sent the text and a new text pops up.

ALYSSA

> She dumped you, Paul. It's over. Move the hell on.

PAUL

> Tell her I'm looking for her

"I guess he wants me to cook, clean, or fuck." I laugh, trying to mask my fear.

I know damn well that nothing is over to Paul until he says it's over. The way he goes from concerned and forgiving to demanding and violent is nothing out of the ordinary, but I've never actually left before. In his mind, he thinks this is just another setback, like any other fight where he can talk his way back into my arms.

The thought of him ever laying a finger on me again sends a chill up my spine. I grab the crochet blanket from the bottom of the bed and toss it around my shoulders, needing its layer of comfort and protection.

I finally take Alyssa's keys and leave the house. I've been taking Alyssa's car to run errands to help Alyssa out because her morning sickness seems to last all day and I don't want to be a burden. Alyssa and Nik are completely happy to have me stay with them, even though this trip seems to no longer have an end date. I just want to be useful, doing anything I can to help out. Which means grabbing whatever foods she craves. No one can keep me from my Chunky Monkey Ben and

Jerry's on my period, so I can't imagine the things hormones do to your cravings while pregnant. I also figured it'd be a good distraction after Paul's texts to Alyssa.

I search everywhere, looking for a damn pickle. It's late and everything seems to close at 6 p.m. Maybe that's the reason Alyssa didn't make the trip out.

Remembering the local gas station, I make my way in that direction, thinking I may be able to get one of those pre-packaged pickles. Hell, if I'm lucky, they will have a gas station deli with a glass jar of oversized dill pickles.

The ancient but somehow modern-looking gas station comes into view, and that's when I hear it. A loud whooshing noise and the flapping sound of rubber on the ground. I may be a taxi and subway kind of girl, but dammit, I know that noise.

A flat fucking tire.

Shit. Shit. Shit.

Okay, just another thing for my bucket list. *I can fix this.* I take out my phone and pull up YouTube. I type: How to change a flat tire. I may be wearing 3-inch heels, but hell if I'm not going to try.

Confident in my teacher, I put my phone in my back pocket and run inside to complete my first mission: The pickle. Thankful for the lackluster gas station deli, I head back to the abandoned car on the side of the road.

I grab the jack and lug wrench from the trunk. I'm sure I look like a complete psychopath. Thank god no one is around to witness this. I'm certain no one has ever looked so happy changing a flat, but I can't help but be proud of myself for attempting something so far out of my wheelhouse. Five minutes ago, I couldn't tell you what a torque wrench was. *Thank you, Youtube.*

Drip.

A water droplet hits the side of my cheek. *Crap.* I look up at the sky in frustration. *Do not fuckin' do it.* I need to hurry or I'm going to get rained on.

I slide the jack under the car, thinking back to my YouTube video. *Loosen the lug nuts, then the jack.* I make my way back to my floppy tire.

Drip.

Drip.

Remember the steps. Loosen, then the Jack, remove, replace. Can't remember exactly what comes after that, but I can watch the video again.

The rain quickly turns into a downpour. The sound of rain pelting against the car echoes in my ears as I rush to finish my second mission.

With my trusty lug wrench, I get to work. Nothing budges. I keep trying, even though most attempts land me right on my ass. I can freakin' do this.

Ten minutes pass and I'm still at step one. "If you weren't so damn tight, we would be done already," I say, losing my last nerve at the stuck bolt. Yet again, my foot slips, sending me backward into a pile of mud off the side of the road. This time, the wrench comes flying out of my hand, landing right on my shin.

In a fit of anger, I kick off my flooded heels and throw them into the car. I'm not only soaking wet, but now covered head to toe in mud.

Okay, this is ridiculous. I even know when to call it quits. There's no way I'm getting these nuts off. I laugh. The smutty books are making even changing a tire sound filthy. Rolling my eyes at my newly perverted mind, I pull out my new phone and scroll through my very diminished contacts list. Not like anyone from my prior list of contacts from the city would be of help thousands of miles away. Nik's out-of-town doing something for the ranch. Alyssa's pregnant, no way. Annabeth, I haven't even seen her outside of the coffee shop yet. Knox's name grabs my attention.

I smirk at the eggplant emoji he put next to his name when he entered his contact. *This man*. I could call Knox. He did say if it's an emergency, he'd be there for me. I suppose this does constitute an emergency.

I click FaceTime to show him my current situation. Instead, before I can flip the camera to the view of my tire, he answers nearly immediately. "What's wrong?"

I'm sure I look disheveled, with mud across my forehead and soaking wet hair.

"I'm fine, but my tire, not so much," I say, laughing before turning the camera on the flat tire.

"Are you changing it yourself? I'll be right there," he says as the screen goes black.

Did he just hang up on me? I didn't even tell him where I was. What the hell? I really thought I'd be able to count on him. I turn around in shock right as Knox's truck pulls alongside my car.

Well, that was quick.

I guess I can count on him.

"I was right across the street. I saw the gas station behind you. Get in," he says, waving toward his truck.

"I can't get the nuts off." I smack the wrench on the deflated tire with a flop.

"So I guess that explains the bare feet," he says deadpan, shaking his head in agreement to himself. "Get in. I'll change the tire."

I just need him to loosen the lug nuts. Then he can go and I continue changing the tire myself. "I want to do this. It's new to my bucket list," I say, my words coming out as a yell over the sound of the rain.

Knox shakes his head and jumps out of the truck before taking the wrench from my hand. "You know, honey, if anyone sees me sitting back just watching you change a tire, I'm going to get a lot of shit for it."

I give him an unamused glare. "I can put my heels back on. I'm sure with being sopping wet, it could fulfill some kind of erotic fantasy of yours. Ya know, make it worth all the shit talkers," I offer and I swear I see the slightest bit of pink in his cheeks, but I can't be sure with the neon coming from the gas station.

Knox begins working, as I grab the spare tire from the trunk and roll it toward the car. He has them loosened by the time I lean the tire against Knox's truck.

Well, shit.

He turns to me and shoots me a devilish grin. Of course, it took him all of a few seconds. That's embarrassing. I put my entire weight into that and not a single budge.

"Have at it, honey. Time for my show." Knox grins, backing up to lean against his truck.

I can't help but notice his V-neck shirt cinching to him from the rain and what is it with a plain black baseball cap on a man? Good god, he could be on the cover of GQ or something.

He gives me a little head nod toward the car, as if to tell me to get to it, before running a hand through his wet brown hair as he lifts his hat to turn it backward. I watch as the beads of rain pour down his face and fall onto his chest.

Fuck me.

I'm not sure what turning a hat backward did, but it made me feel all sorts of things. I wouldn't admit it out loud, but boy oh boy, do I have a crush on Knox Hayes.

For an outsider, one might think I didn't have time to grieve my past relationship or that I moved on too fast. The truth is, though, I've known I haven't been in love with Paul for a very long time. There isn't one thing I can say that I miss about him. I guess that makes sense being our relationship was so one sided.

I remove the loosened lug nuts, jack the car up, and remove the tire. I think knowing Knox's eyes are on me gives me some kind of superhuman strength, not wanting to look like a damsel in distress.

I can feel the heat from his stare combing over my body as I lift the spare on. I'm seriously impressed that I just changed a tire. Well, with some help. I turn swiftly to share my excitement, my foot slipping from beneath me in the mud. Before I can process that I am about to fall flat on my ass for the umpteeth time, Knox pushes himself off from the truck and his hands grip me by the waist. My breath hitches as his touch sears the skin beneath my shirt.

"Thank you for fulfilling my fantasies, but I'm going to take it from here." Knox's voice is rough and low as his hands remain on me.

He's not asking me this time, he's telling me. So, I let him go about finishing the job. I got to use the jack; that's all I really wanted. I'll still be crossing this off my bucket list and consider this as a job well done.

Chapter Thirteen

Knox

I peek at Haylee sitting in my truck, avoiding the rain as I finish lowering the jack. When I saw a FaceTime from her, nerves coursed through me. Sure, we see each other every day, but I had given her my number in case of an emergency.

I admit I've been hoping she would shoot me a text or spontaneous phone call, but that hasn't been the case. This wasn't what I had in mind, even though I'm happy to be her knight in shining armor.

When she said she had a flat and I saw her covered in mud, fear spread through me, but the moment I pulled my truck next to her, I felt a shiver of excitement down my spine.

Haylee was wearing a white t-shirt with black jeans that looked like they were painted on and not by the rain. Her bare feet were sinking in the mud that ran up her legs, across her see-through shirt, and streaking across her face. Goddamn, it may have been one of the hottest sights.

Luckily, no one else had been around to spot her. Not only because it gave her reason to need me, but also there are some absolute creeps around here.

Once I got the lug nuts off, she was determined to finish putting the tire on by herself, so I sat back and watched until I told her to hang tight in my truck. She was not wrong. She unlocked an entirely new fantasy for me. I'm not sure if it was her changing a tire, being covered in mud, or her need for independence. Whatever it was, it was sexy as hell.

I sling the destroyed tire into the bed of my truck, then head to my gym bag in the back seat of the cab. Quickly, I pull my soaking wet shirt over my head and toss it on the floor. Making my way back to the driver's seat, I can feel Haylee's eyes burning through me.

"Should be all set," I confirm, shutting the door as I place the bag of gym clothes in my lap and taking out the first shirt I see.

"Really, Knox, thank you so much. You're a lifesaver," she praises.

My eyes trace her body, soaked head to toe, covered in mud as her shirt clings to her curves.

"Sooo worth it."

She lets out the softest. I wonder if that's a similar noise to what she'd sound like if I were tracing my tongue up the inside of her thigh.

"We are disgusting," she says, interrupting my train of thought as she opens the mirror on the visor. She runs her hands over her hair and wipes at the mud on her face.

"Here, put these on before you get back into Alyssa's car like that. She won't care much about the tire, but mud, now that's another story."

I hand her a sweatshirt and shorts from my bag before pulling a clean shirt over my head. "She's such a neat freak, isn't she?" she asks, lifting her tank top over her head.

"Not here!" I groan, grabbing her hand that's pulling the hem of her shirt up. She shrugs at me, like undressing in my truck on the side of a road is completely normal. To my surprise, she continues to undress.

She is going to be the death of me. It's dark, but I can still make out every detail. I'd like to think I'm a gentleman, but I can't help but take her in. Haylee's bra is white and all lace, accentuating her tanned skin. Her nipples are hard from the cold and peeking through her bra, daring my lips to warm them.

"You saw me in my bathing suit." She shakes her head like it's no big deal. Shirtless, she begins to slide down her wet pants as if the thong on my passenger seat covers more of her ass than her bikini did. I bite my knuckles on my clenched fist, quietly admiring her wearing nothing but a bra and thong in the front seat of my truck. Right now, I want nothing but to worship every inch of her body.

"Fuck, Haylee. This is nothing like you in a bikini."

She grabs my USMC crewneck sweatshirt and pulls it over her head. "Well, then take the show as a thank you for helping me out."

"Okay. Well, in that case . . . "

I slowly run my hand up her side, dragging the sweatshirt up with the movement. Her eyes bore into mine as my palm encompasses her tiny frame. My dick twitching as my hand traces over the white lace that is forever etched into my mind. I take note of the rapid movement of her ribs beneath my touch before I shift the sweatshirt over her breasts.

Breaking the intimate moment, she laughs, pushing me away as she guides my sweatshirt back down. I love how playful she is—it's refreshing. Her eyes meet mine again and she ever so slightly bites her bottom lip as she slips her hand behind her back and pulls her bra out through her sleeve in one full motion before tossing it in the backseat with her pants. My dick pulsates in my jeans.

She looks like a fucking dream.

In my sweatshirt.

Braless.

Bare-assed.

In my fuckin' truck.

"For fuck's sake, honey. Do you even know what you're doing to me?" I wipe at a smear of dirt from her lip. "If you're going to strip naked in my truck, it's going to be because you can't wait another second to have my dick inside you, got it?"

Haylee's hand grips my thigh, looking down at the massive hard on I'm sporting. I swear I can just look at her and be hard as a rock. She leans in and gently feathers her lips over my ear. "Maybe another time."

Fuck.

Chapter Fourteen
Knox

NIK

Melanie's here.

KNOX

Not interested.

NIK

Really?

KNOX

Really.

NIK

Why not? Would it have anything to do with a certain sister-in-law of mine that I saw wearing your sweatshirt?

The Broken Spoke—it's the only bar in town and our normal spot for a Friday night. Tonight, there is a band playing, so it's more crowded than usual. Walking in, I immediately spot Nik waiting in our usual spot—a high top in the corner nearest the door and bar.

I make eyes with the bartender Max and throw her a nod. She grabs a glass and pours me my favorite beer from the tap before I even take my seat. One of the perks of being a usual.

Nik's telling me about his and Alyssa's trip out of town for a friend's wedding this weekend and explaining to me what needs to be taken care of on the ranch. As if I haven't been running it with him for the past ten years. I nod and listen, knowing he's going to tell me either way.

"I'm also going to need you to watch out for Haylee." The mention of her immediately pulls my trance away from Haylee and Alyssa on the other side of the bar. Haylee, who looks to be drinking a beer. *Why the fuck is she drinking?*

"Of course, Nik."

Our conversation pauses as Max approaches with another round. She gives me a quick wink before heading back to the bar.

"Alyssa doesn't even want to go. She knows Paul is looking for Haylee and wouldn't be surprised if he shows up after what happened," he says a bit too nonchalantly.

"Looking for her?" I question, maybe a bit more angrily than I should. "What do you mean after what happened? I thought *he* was the one that broke into *her* apartment? What's that asshole got to be pissed about?" She should be going after him.

I study Alyssa and Haylee, who are now playing pool in the back of the bar. I can tell Haylee is drunk when she drops the chalk to the cue. A sober Alyssa is laughing at her side. I smile at my realization; I should've known from the start when we went cliff jumping. Alyssa is the one who's pregnant.

"He broke in looking for an engagement ring he planned to propose with. Hay found it first and mailed it to him at his job. Guess he's fucking pissed."

A ring?

He was going to propose?

My eyes dart back to the girls laughing and fumbling with the pool sticks, occupying the one and only table from a group of guys clearly waiting for their turn.

There's no way she would've said yes.

Would she?

"Knox, I'm sorry to put this on you, but you need to know in case he shows up. He's abusive. The last time Haylee was with him, he threatened her with a gun."

My eyes snap from Haylee back to Nik. Blood rushes through my veins. This isn't new information, but hearing it again sends a violent pulsation through my body.

"He will have to kill me first before I let him touch her again."

My response might've been a bit too over the top, because Nik lifts his beer toward me in cheers.

"Well, this explains not being interested in Melanie." Laughing, he points his finger at me, "Oh, and he's a cop."

Now that. That, I did *not* know.

"Fucking great. An arrogant asshole with a gun and a badge."

He laid his hands on *her*. I can't help but think of how scared she must've been, as to why she never called the police, and why she looks as though she carries a world of pain.

"Alright, buddy, time to round the girls up and get out of here."

Nik is also staring at the guys making small talk with the girls. One chatting up Alyssa and the other has his hand on Haylee's shoulder, trying to whisper in her ear. When he puts his hand on her, I notice the tremble run through her as she sucks in a breath.

I see red and I'm out of my seat and by her side before I can think twice.

"Hands off, buddy."

The men glare at one another hesitantly. Hand still on

Haylee, his eyes size me up. Knowing he and his beer belly aren't up for the task, he backs away.

Haylee's fear washes away as she gives me an excited smile, not having known I've been here this whole time. She leaps toward me with her arms open for a hug. I lift her as she wraps her legs around my body and she dangles her arms around my neck. As if it's the most natural thing in the world. She lets out a giggle I feel through my entire body.

Since getting to know her, I've been completely mesmerized by her. I can't help but notice the short flowing dress she's wearing and her cowgirl boots in place of the heels against my back. She's giddy and drunk and she's in *my* arms.

"Let's get drinks! Ugh, maybe pee first, though." She bursts into another giggle fit. I begin walking down the hallway toward the restrooms. Her legs, still tightly wrapped around me.

"No drinks. It's time to go, honey. Use the restroom and I'll meet you back here."

She frowns, swipes for my hat, and places it on her head. Damn, she looks good in my hat. Holding her up with one arm, I press her back against the wall of the hallway with my body, and Haylee lets out a quiet gasp. Not like the ones I've seen from her in the past, like the asshole from moments ago whose ass I'd love to kick. I cradle the side of her head and graze my thumb along her cheekbone, searching her eyes for any trace of panic.

Pure elation.

I press my body firmly against hers. Thrilled at the sensation, she lets out an exhale that brushes my neck. My dick tightens against my jeans, which I am certain she can feel pressed into her.

I give her a playful stern grin before whispering, "You know what they say, wear the hat, ride the cowboy."

I lean my head closer toward her and bite her earlobe,

placing a kiss on her neck. She rocks against my length in search of friction. I can't resist her anymore. This beautiful and resilient woman has gotten to me. Knowing she's not pregnant somehow allows me to forge ahead with all the things I've been dying to do.

"I know the rule." She shoots me a wink.

I press my straining dick to her center as a warning, giving her the bit of pleasure she craves. Her arms clutch around my neck as she grinds against me. I hold her up with ease, allowing her to take what she needs.

"Good girl. You like how my dick feels against your pussy?"

A moan escapes as her breathing intensifies.

My lips trail kisses along her neck and down her collarbone as my hands grip firmly on her ass beneath her dress.

"I bet you are just soaking wet for me, aren't you, honey?" Her head tilts back in ecstasy. My dick is straining against my jeans as it rubs the fabric of her thong under her dress.

"Take what you need, Haylee. Show me exactly how you make that perfect little pussy come for me."

To my surprise, Haylee's hand slides from behind my neck and dives into her panties. Her nails dig into my neck as she rubs quick circles over her clit. Her head leans forward into my chest, muffling her moans as she comes.

Fuck.

I wish she wasn't drunk, so I can touch her the way I really want. I've already taken more than I should with her right now. I don't think she'd appreciate being fucked in the hallway of a bar while she's drunk.

Her breathing slows, and she pulls her hand from her panties. My hand catches hers and I guide her fingers into my mouth, savoring the sweet taste.

"Mmmm . . . honey. You taste so good for me."

I release her gently, putting her back on wobbly feet, and

adjusting her dress. She steps back toward the restroom and with my hat still on her head, she tips it farewell with a wink.

I quickly tuck the massive hard on I'm sporting into my waistband before heading back to the bar. "Got her?" Nik says, throwing me a head nod toward the ladies' room.

"Yeah man, get Alyssa home. I've got her."

I know he thinks he's trying to stick me and Haylee together every chance he gets, something I am not in the least bit mad about. I'm sure Alyssa's behind it somehow, too. They'd love to know that Haylee just came all over my jeans. The thought alone does nothing to tame the massive hard on flipped into my belt.

"I don't feel so good," Haylee cautions as I turn onto the dirt path of the ranch.

I know I saw her take a few shots and down a couple beers. Who the hell knows what she had before I got there. I crack the window, hoping the fresh air will help the nausea pass.

She's sitting in the middle seat of the truck, her leg grazing mine. She was too drunk to care what side was what when getting in and her bag, the size of a toddler, took up the passenger seat.

"You're okay, honey, we're almost . . . " interrupted by the sound of hurling. I look down at me and Haylee covered in vomit. Rolling the windows down, I try to focus on my hand rubbing Haylee's back, not the smell of vomit.

We pull down the gravel driveway, which is shared by the main house and the cottage. The cottage is set back further. It's small and comfortable. It's home. I drive past Nik and Alyssa's house, seeing all the lights out.

They don't need to deal with this.

She's leaning against me in my seat. I pick her up and pull her out of the truck. Before her feet hit the ground, she's heaving yet again. This has to be karma for hitting on her when I thought she was pregnant.

I hold her hair back, even though she's already covered in vomit, so there isn't much of a point. Haylee looks up at me with watery eyes. "I'm so sorry."

"It's okay, it happens to the best of us, honey," I reassure her, rubbing her back a few more times. I then carry her inside to the bathroom.

"Shower . . . I'll be right outside if you need anything."

Haylee looks at me with a sorry frown and I run my finger beneath a fallen tear before shutting the door behind me.

I gather everything she might need. A pair of my sweats, a shirt, and an extra toothbrush. I knock twice on the door. "Haylee, I left you a towel and clean clothes outside the door."

I hear her fumbling around in the shower. From the sound of it, every shampoo and conditioner bottle got knocked into the bottom of the tub.

I put my hand to my temples, already regretting the words about to come from my mouth. "Do you need help?"

I have a sister and know I would like someone to care for her if she were in this situation. I'm not sure if they were in the shower, though.

I've seen plenty of women naked. I'm a grown ass man. I can look at her body in a non-sexual way.

Right?

"I got the spins, I . . . I . . . don't feel too good."

I hesitate, my hand on the doorknob.

"Knox, I'm naked," Haylee admits, pointing out the obvious that I am all too aware of at the moment.

"Nothing I haven't seen before, honey." I walk in with her change of clothes and toothbrush in hand, laying them on the vanity. She's just under the spray from the shower head, her forehead placed on her wrist, leaning against the wall.

She's nothing like what I've seen before. Glistening skin, tan line just around her breast, waxed head to toe. I'm a moth to a flame. Haylee begins to turn toward me as her eyes slowly open. She's got to be mortified. This is nothing like her partially naked in my truck. I take off my puke covered shirt and give her a reassuring smirk.

"It's okay. I got it," I tell her, reaching down for the shampoo bottle. I run the shampoo through her long brown hair, trying my best to not marvel at the sight of her with her head tipped back and eyes closed as I massage her scalp. Leaning her head into my every touch with gentle sighs.

I grab my loofa and squeeze soap onto it. This really is some kind of screwed up karma.

She holds onto my shoulders, her bare breast directly in my line of sight. Just an inch or two closer, my mouth could be on them.

She's absolutely breathtaking. Curved hips and dimples right above her full ass. Flawless tits that would fit perfectly in my hands. I run the loofa over her chest, then her arms, then to her stomach and down her smooth legs before rinsing her clean.

I turn off the water and grab two towels. I wrap one over her shoulders and the other I use to dry her hair. "Thank you," she says hesitantly, breaking the silence and stepping out of the shower. "I was fine until I got into the truck." A look of horror spreads across her face. "Oh my god, Knox, your truck! I'll go clean it!" I hand her the clothes and toothbrush.

"No, you won't. I don't want you to worry about it. Put these on and I'll show you where you can sleep tonight."

Once she's done getting dressed and brushing her teeth, I make sure she is comfortable in my bed. I spend a good hour scrubbing out my truck before passing out on the couch.

It wasn't long before my thoughts of Haylee turned into the usual night terror. Scrubbing the shit night's sleep from my eyes, I get up and make myself a coffee, being sure to be quiet and not wake Haylee. Not my normal espresso, but I'm not leaving her here alone if she doesn't remember what happened last night.

I carry my coffee to the bathroom, sitting it on the vanity. I step into the shower, needing to wake myself up after the rough night. I can't help but think of Haylee's perfectly bare pussy and hard nipples wet in my shower.

This shower.

I stiffen at the thought of my hands washing over her body. I fist my dick in my hand. I shouldn't. She's just in the other room, the thought making me even more turned on.

I close my eyes and stroke slowly, picturing her naked body. The feel of my hand grazing her smooth skin. I continue to pump myself. I imagine her face looking down at me while I washed her, my head right between her legs.

I hear the door open and my eyes shoot open.

Shit.

I freeze, and my hand stops at the base of my shaft. My pulse races at Haylee barging in on me jerking off.

She's wearing my shirt, which hits her mid-thigh. Her hair is a wavy mess in a bun on top of her head. She cocks her head to the side, her eyes studying me through the half glass wall.

Why is my hand still on my dick?

A playful smile forms across her face.

Good girl.

Anyone else would've sneaked out the front door after the mess she made last night. "Good morning," she says with a wink, hopping up on the vanity and taking my fresh coffee to her lips, her eyes glued to my cock. I tighten my grip at the base of my cock.

"You going to watch, honey," I say, masking the nerves of

being caught. I get even harder at the realization she purpose-fully walked in on me.

"I think that's only fair after last night."

Fuckin' hell.

I run my hand up and down my length, searching for relief. The sight of her watching me, her eyes fixated on my dick as she so confidently sits on the vanity, has me tightening my grip. If she wants to watch, the hell if I'm going to stop her.

She places the coffee down beside her. Eyes glued to mine, her tongue glides across her bottom lip before biting it.

"Fuck," I grunt. I want her so fuckin' bad.

She slides off the counter and walks toward me. She lifts my shirt over her head, exposing her naked body. I pump myself faster as my eyes trace over her exposed body. Stepping into the shower, I marvel all over again at the water rolling down her curves. Reaching around me, she grabs the bar of soap on the ledge. From behind me, she runs the soap along the bare skin of my chest.

Haylee moves down toward my stomach to the V at my waist, then back up. Repeating the path a few more times, she begins to make her way down my arm that's bracing the wall.

"Haylee, honey," I let out a moan while I continue to pump my dick. I'm going to come. I'm in my shower, jerking off, and I'm going to come just at her touch. She places the bar of soap to the side and her wet, naked body presses against my back. Her lips kiss the back of my shoulder.

"Is this what you want?" Haylee whispers. I can't get words out. I let out another long moan. Taking that as a yes, her hand glides down my arm slowly, placing her hand over mine that fists my erection. She tightens her hand, making me grip myself firmer.

"Were you in here, with your hand on your cock, thinking

of fucking me while I was asleep in the other room?" Her voice is delicate and fuck, this girl's got a dirty mouth.

"Fuck . . . Yes, Haylee." I let out another moan. "I always think of you."

With her hand mimicking mine, she makes me stroke faster. I don't even think I have gotten a hand job since high school, but something about this, her barely touching me, is the most intimate I have ever been with a woman.

"I think of you too," she whispers.

"Haylee, I'm going to come," I grit, tilting my head back. "Fuck, honey. Yes."

Shivers run through me, rocking against her as I spill myself onto the shower floor. Her lips meet my neck, sending another shake throughout my body. Dropping her hands, she steps aside, walking out of the shower. Then throws my shirt back on and turns to me. "For the hat," she says with a smile, shutting the door behind her.

I sink back to the shower wall and melt down into the floor. What the fuck? How did this happen? She's nothing like I thought. She's spontaneous, courageous, thoughtful, beautiful. Goddamn perfect.

Chapter Fifteen
Haylee

I can't believe I threw up. On Knox, no less. He was so understanding and caring. Even after washing chunks of vomit out of my hair, he still was a perfect gentleman. The thought alone makes me smile, no matter how embarrassed I might be. He's a saint. I don't know many men who wouldn't blink an eye at being vomited on and proceed to wash the girl's hair.

I never drink in excess, but in the spirit of trying new things and thinking about me for once, I got drunk. Alyssa may have thought I could handle more than I could, though. Sue me. People my age drink like that most weekends.

What *I am* unsure of is if they grind all over their brother-in-law's best friend. As innocent as it might have been, it was by far the hottest thing I have experienced.

After dry humping Knox, I camped out in the restroom for a bit. I downed the two shooters Alyssa had coerced me into putting in my purse. What I assumed would help calm me from my *Oh Shit* moment, only made me teeter totter from happily buzzed to wasted.

Being the gentleman he is, Knox put me in his bed and

headed to the couch. Even as heated as our moment at the bar was, he didn't take it any further. Hell, he didn't even kiss me.

Waking up—encased in his scent, I felt more at ease than I have in years. It was like my body had a mind of its own once I heard his shower turn on. I'd spent a few nights with my vibrator picturing Knox thrusting over me if I'm being honest. He makes me feel safe and worthy. So, I pretended I had all the confidence in the world. Internally, I was a nervous mess until I walked in and saw him way ahead of me.

Watching him firmly run his hand up and down his thick length as his eyes locked with mine, wearing nothing but a sexy grin, washed away any doubt I may have had.

God, it was like nothing I've experienced.

I haven't been with anyone besides Paul in years, but the connection Knox and I shared . . . that was a first. Which is why once he came, I bolted. The moment my hands grazed his body, I knew I had mistaken our relationship as pure sexual tension.

Am I ready for something more? I am being pulled toward him, but there is also a part of me afraid to give in to that. From the moment he got to the bar, I felt safe again. Hell, since the moment we first met. Being near him sends a current of electricity through me—roaring butterflies in my stomach. I feel protected, seen, and respected. Everything I have longed for.

HAYLEE

Thank you for last night.

KNOX

Thank you for this morning.

HAYLEE

My pleasure ;)

KNOX

You're going to be the death of me, honey.

I'm curled up on the guestroom bed, popping two Advil into my mouth. Alyssa's curled up next to me, listening to me ramble on about my escapades at the Broken Spoke.

"You've always been a lightweight," Alyssa says, rolling her eyes.

I had told her about the moment in the hall, and I swear she is secretly planning a wedding in her head. She had screeched so loud that Nik came barreling into the room. I can't imagine what her reaction would be if I told her about both incidents in the shower.

Alyssa rolls toward me, her hands clasped together against her cheek. "We will be back Monday morning. It's just two nights. If you need anything at all, I want you to call us."

She's on edge after Paul's text. I sit up and plaster on a forced smile. I know she'd stay if I asked. "I'll be fine. Go. Have fun."

In all honesty, I'm just counting down the minutes for him to find me here. Having Alyssa and Nik under the same roof provided a small sense of comfort that I didn't realize I needed.

Every other text message or voicemail before Knox got me my new phone just solidified it. Paul would start the day texting about how he needs me back and loves me. His life just isn't the same without me. Then by the time it was happy hour, it was that I'm a bitch or a good-for-nothing cunt.

"Knox will be around too, ya know." She hits me with a devious grin as she sits, fluffing the pillow behind her.

I pick up a pillow off the end of the bed and throw it at her laughing. The nostalgia hits me full force. I've missed having my sister.

"Seriously, go. Everything will be fine. You two need time away."

"I decided I'm telling Nik tonight once we get to the hotel," she says gleaming.

"The doctor said the baby looks perfect, but after the last time, I know I won't fully be relaxed until the three of us are home from the hospital."

I give her a smile and squeeze her hand, thinking back on the heartbreak she endured. They tried for so long. Then it was all gone.

"I know it's easier said than done, but don't worry unless you have to. If the doctor said the baby is healthy, then they're healthy. Don't try to convince yourself otherwise. You're going to be an amazing mom, Alyssa."

"Thanks, Hay. I'd be even better having you here through it all. I know your job lets you work remotely and the only reason you went to the office was to get away from *him*. But our offer is still on the table. We would really like it if you would come stay with us."

I'm not sure why her offer surprises me. It has come up in the past every time I called her after a fight. Now, though, the offer has me contemplating if that actually is what I want.

"You could start fresh. We can see each other more than a few times a year. Plus, you can babysit!" She gives me a thumbs up like there aren't a million other things to consider.

I would love nothing more than to see my sister every day and be involved in my niece or nephew's life. The thought of not seeing Knox everyday feels like a brick in my stomach.

"I did talk to Eileen about more time out here and she just laughed and told me my job's remote." I give her a sideways smirk. "It's just that my entire life is in New York. It's home."

I look around the room I've now referred to as home on more than one occasion. My clothes hang in the closet, dried flowers from the farmers market hanging upside down, a stack of books piled near the window seat, pictures littering my mirror of the short time I've been here. One in particular catches my eye first. I had just ridden my first horse. Knox's hands are placed on each side of my hips. I'm smiling ear-to-ear in laughter, looking at Alyssa taking the picture while Knox's eyes burn into me.

I so much want to scream out, "Yes!" I feel more myself here than I've ever felt. It's the first time in my life I'm not worried about anyone's opinion other than my own. It's not the fear of up and leaving my entire life. I mean, I didn't have much of a life in New York to begin with.

It's the fear of up and moving my entire life to Texas and pieces of my life following me here. I'm afraid of putting everyone in Paul's war path. I just can't fathom anyone I love getting hurt because of me and my poor choices.

I chickened out. I'm not used to being alone in that big of a house with every noise making me think Paul's going to walk right through the door. My apartment never felt like home. I was always walking on eggshells, never knowing what would make him snap.

Alyssa and Nik's feels more like home than my apartment in the city ever has. For whatever reason, I have that gut feeling that everything is going to shatter in pieces around me. I can feel it, the shiver that runs straight to your bones and makes your heart drop to your stomach. It's only a matter of time. No matter how much comfort I normally find in their house, I just can't seem to find it tonight.

God, this is stupid.

I'm a full ass adult afraid to be home alone.

I'm reading the instructions on how to set up the tent. I

only have maybe thirty minutes left of daylight. I couldn't even watch a movie without jumping every second at the creaking pipes. So, yet another thing I'm crossing off my list. Camping. Plus, who would suspect me to be camped right outside?

KNOX

What the hell are you doing, honey?

HAYLEE

Setting up a tent. What's it look like?

KNOX

Like you have no idea what you're doing.

"City girl's camp?" Knox's voice sends instant relief through me as he walks toward me. Since day one of his presence, he provides me with a sense of security. He's wearing gray sweats and a white v-neck t-shirt.

Not the gray fuckin' sweats, man.

I laugh, looking at my campsite and back at him with my hand holding the instructions up in confusion.

"Apparently not. I have no idea what I'm doing."

I turn my head toward my sad excuse for a campsite. My cheeks heat up at the image of him from this morning gripping his dick, eyeing me like I was a meal.

Knox opens a blanket and lays it out on the grass. He instructs me to sit and I do just that. Assembling a tent—not on my bucket list. I watch as he assembles it with far less effort than it took me.

I don't hide the fact that I am checking him out the entire time, either. Every time he sees me eyeing him up, he gives me a smirk or a devilish wink.

He loves it just as much as I do.

Knox grabs another blanket and throws it around my shoulders, taking a seat next to me.

"Why are we camping?"

I take a minute to think. "The truth?" I ask him, not having been able to come up with any good explanation.

He looks at me with a questioning stare. "I always want the truth from you. You don't need to pretend with me, Haylee."

I let out an audible sigh, falling back onto the blanket. He truly sees me, my practiced facade and all. Knox copies my movements. "Well, remember my ex? Paul? He's looking for me, and I doubt to just talk. I was scared inside. So . . . I figured no one would look for me in a tent behind the house."

Taking in Knox's body language, he does not look pleased. Is he pissed? Jesus, he just set up a tent because I am acting like a scared little kid camping out. I break the silence. "Now that I say it out loud, it sounds so stupid. I'm sure you had something better to do than set up a tent. I'm sorry."

I look up at the stars. Embarrassed at my truth.

"Haylee," he says my name firmly, but it sounds like velvet as he pulls me into his side. "I find absolutely nothing stupid about you not feeling safe. I would set up a tent for you every single night if it meant you felt safe."

I can't help it when a tear rolls down my cheek, and he gently brushes it away with his thumb. The people who were supposed to protect me, they all failed me. Mom, Dad, Paul. But here's Knox, who has no reason to, but continues to keep making me feel safer than I've ever felt.

Another tear falls, but now for a completely different reason.

For Christ's sake, I keep crying in front of this man. He's going to think I'm a lunatic.

"Truth?" This time he asks, wiping another tear from my cheek.

I'm not sure what other truths there are to tell. I'm pretty positive I just unloaded all I've got on him. I nod my head.

"Up until yesterday, when I put two and two together at the bar, I thought you were pregnant," Knox says, giving me a cheesy grin in embarrassment.

He thought I was pregnant?!

What the fuck?

I sit up, completely shocked by his truth. "Pregnant?" I question.

A few seconds pass while I collect my thoughts. He turns and places his head in his palm, looking up at me.

"Just to confirm for you . . . no. I'm not pregnant, Knox. What made you think that?" I say with an awkward laugh.

"The pregnancy test you bought, the prenatal vitamins in the kitchen." He points toward the house.

I completely forgot I had bought that test for Alyssa. My mind was too caught up in her. I never stopped for a second to think if Knox thought it was mine.

"Knox, those are Alyssa's. She is pregnant," I admit.

"I figured that out too," he says with an embarrassed laugh.

A moment passes before he looks up at the stars appreciatively, his eyes landing back on mine. "And she's good? The baby . . . the baby is good?"

I know what he's asking, his face tight with concern. I'm sure Nik had told him about Alyssa miscarrying last year. "Yes, everyone is good."

He smiles ear-to-ear and jumps up in excitement, pulling me to my feet along with him. He wraps me up in a hug and spins me out and back into his arms, dancing to the crickets and the sound of our laughter. With one hand on my hip and the other in my hand, we rock to the sound of cicadas.

I grin at his excitement. I love that Alyssa has someone like Knox in her corner cheering her on.

My mind begins to go back to his truth.

He thought I was pregnant?

This whole time?!

"So, you thought I was pregnant this entire time?" I question, freezing in place, the words coming from me harshly. His hands drop to his sides as I step back, putting distance between us. I immediately regret the action, losing the comforting warmth he provided.

Is this why he's been so nice and compassionate? Pity?

He thinks, letting several moments pass.

I'm not sure if I should be flattered or slightly weirded out. We've spent a lot of time together. I mean, we were close enough at this point that I let him shower me while I was shit-faced, then basically jerked him off.

"What? What was this? Do you have some pregnancy fetish?" I say with a cringe worthy laugh.

We've been flirting with each other for weeks. The only difference is he thought I was carrying another man's child. It's kinda weird, even if he figured out I was, in fact, not pregnant yesterday before our shower incident.

He steps toward me, running his hand from my wrist to my hand. His eyes search mine as if he's trying to determine what to say next.

"Haylee, you have to understand. You were everything I wasn't expecting. You came into my life like a fucking tornado. I had this picture of you in my mind. Alyssa's little sister from New York City. You were supposed to be spoiled, arrogant, and conceited," he says, describing what Paul has told me time and time again.

His voice is angry and firm with frustration. "I *thought* you were those things. Things I told myself because the moment I first saw you, I knew you had the ability to completely destroy me. But these past few weeks, I've gotten to know the real you. Your independence, your strength, your wit, your humor, the way you curse like a trucker. Jesus, even the goddamn cowgirl boots with the sundresses. I can't get enough of it, Haylee.

Enough of *you*. I want to fuckin' drown myself in it. So, no. The fact that I may have thought you were pregnant up until last night . . . no. No, Haylee. It didn't stop me from wanting you because I didn't have much of a choice."

Before I can speak, he pulls me in and our lips crash together as his hands firmly run up and down my body. His wet tongue glides over mine as our kiss deepens. He tastes like espresso and I can't help but moan into him as he deepens the kiss.

Being told the exact opposite of what's been drilled into my head for years feels like a damn weight has lifted off my shoulders. Knowing he'd want me in the middle of my very worst, on the run and pregnant, only solidifies our connection.

I want so badly to give him everything. It would be so easy with him. So easy to become too comfortable.

But I can't.

"Knox," my lips tread over his between my words, "I can't." I instantly regret my words, but I know better.

He runs his hand through a loose strand of hair, tucking it back into place, and kisses my forehead. His breath lingers there for a moment. "I'm sorry." Then a kiss to the same spot seals his words.

We stand there, our eyes searching one another's. We both know this is something, but what could ever come of it?

His hand laces mine and he pulls me to the blanket, positioning me between his legs. His arms encase me and his thumb traces against the inside of my splayed-out palm.

We stay quiet. There's an electricity between us I've never felt before.

The fact that he still wants me after confessing the most gruesome of details about my relationship with Paul and thinking I was pregnant with another man's child. I'm not sure what he expects out of whatever the hell it is we are doing.

I'm not ready for more. I can't be. I just ended the worst fucking relationship in history. Hell, if Paul found out about Knox . . .

He'd kill him.

Actually kill him.

I can't.

What am I doing?

I finally break our silence. "I live two thousand miles away."

"I know," Knox replies.

"Everything with Paul is . . . " I let out an exasperated sigh.

"I know that too," Knox says, gripping my hand and giving it a squeeze.

This can't happen. No matter how right it feels.

We spend the rest of the night telling stories, catching lightning bugs, and making s'mores. Knox thought I needed the true camping experience.

We don't sleep in the tent Knox set up for me. Instead, we go back into the house and gather every single blanket and pillow to lay out under the stars. Knox chases me up and down the halls, room to room, like two children on the playground, threatening to get me sticky with his s'more-covered fingers.

When we get to the living room, he tosses me onto the couch, tickles me, and gives me another kiss. But this time to my forehead and it pulsates through every inch of my body. I feel his arousal straining against his sweats as he pushes into me.

His eyes search mine. I know what he wants.

Hell, what *I* want.

"You know I can't." I instantly regret speaking.

I want him. But there's too much baggage. Too much distance. Nothing past one night, and I know that I can't have just one night with Knox. I need so much more.

Knox doesn't respond; he just lifts me up, throws me over his shoulder with a spank to my ass, and carries me back outside. We spend the rest of the night curled under the stars, wrapped in a dozen pillows and blankets.

For the first time, I slept well. Not once waking in fear for my life. Falling asleep and waking up to Knox's arms wrapped around me is all the comfort I need.

It all feels so right.

So normal.

ism*Chapter Sixteen*

Knox

It's been all day and I still can't stop thinking of her lips on mine. One taste and I was addicted: hearing her moan as I bit her bottom lip, feeling her hands wrapped around my neck, inhaling her citrus scent that was uniquely hers. Everything about her draws me to her.

I'll admit when I woke up, with her face nuzzled into the crook of my arm and leg sprawled over my body, I laid there soaking up every ounce of Haylee. Watching her eyes flutter as she dreamed, the rise of the sun casting on her delicate skin, to the soft rise and fall of her chest with every breath. I was captivated.

She has friends, family, and a career in New York. Even if Paul didn't instill such fear in her, it's not like she'd uproot her entire life for me. To what? Date me?

I just know I want her.

I need her.

I fucking crave her.

The stab to the heart pierces through me, a cruel reminder

of the pain I've felt too many times. A part of me wishes I told her to fuck Paul and fuck the distance.

What is wrong with me? Usually, I can sleep with a woman and not think twice.

All I did was kiss Haylee and I'm a freakin' goner.

I come back to the cottage after a day of work to find Melanie at my front porch. She's here for a booty call. She's made that *very* clear with her obsessive text messaging.

Haylee turned *me* down. Not because we both didn't want each other, but because of the baggage she *thinks* she comes with. Maybe I am just fixated on her because I need to get laid.

Hell, it's been a-freakin-while.

If I just fuck Melanie, I'll be able to get whatever this infatuation is out of my system. I invite her in for a drink.

Multiple glasses of whiskey later, I am regretting my decision. I used to get a hard on just looking at Melanie, and now watching her striptease in front of me from the comfort of my couch, I feel nothing. For whatever reason, my traitor dick is telling me no.

I can't help but feel like I'm being unfaithful.

Unfaithful to a girl who turned me down.

Fuck. I run my hand over my face. I can't believe I'm going to do this. *I am such an asshole.* "Melanie, you know you're gorgeous, right?"

She looks at me and winks, wearing nothing but a neon pink thong and matching bra as she sways to the music. She looks like a goddamn highlighter. What self-respecting thirty-something year old wears neon? I think about what Haylee's panties and bras look like. I doubt any of them resemble highlighters.

"Can you sit down?" I grab her tank top and jeans, handing them to her. Obviously telling her to dress herself. "I'm so sorry, I just . . . I can't. I think there's someone else.

You don't deserve this." I rake my hand through my hair in frustration. "I am so sorry. I'm a complete ass."

I've never felt worse about myself than I do at this moment. I could've figured this out on my front porch, but I had to go ahead and talk myself into sleeping with her, as if that would downplay my feelings for Haylee.

Yeah, right.

Melanie's half naked and I'm turning her down, *again*. What has Haylee freakin' done to me?

No woman deserves this. Even if my dick did give a fuck about Melanie, she doesn't deserve me fucking her while I think of another woman.

"Do you want to talk about it, sweetie?" she says, pulling on her jeans and tank top. "I'm a really good listener, ya know."

I let it all out to the poor woman. I explain everything that's happened since the moment Haylee arrived. The pregnancy test, the obsessive texts from her abusive ex, the break-in, my insane crush, and how I ultimately arrived here. All the while, she's half naked, turned down, and listening to me go on about another woman. *I really am an asshole.*

I don't think I would have the class to sit through this if roles were reversed, but she doesn't show a hint of remorse for asking if I'd like to talk. She has never been one to be shy, so I'm certain she'd let me know. *Clearly.*

Melanie tells me about how she was with someone who was abusive. Not in the same way as Haylee, but verbally and how it took her a long time to realize she deserved good things. She explains the trauma it leaves you with. The constant thought of failure, and never being good enough. Simply all around undeserving.

She makes a good point that Haylee doesn't seem like the person who would drag me into her life if she thought it could cause more disruption in either of our lives, especially being that Paul seems to be a danger.

After an innocent peck to Melanie's cheek and walking her to her car, I sit outside with my thoughts.

Maybe she just thinks she's going to drag me down with her and that somehow I will end up in Paul's line of fire, too. She's a smart girl. Paul wouldn't just have repercussions for her. I think she thought not putting our emotions into action was the best for both of us at that moment. No matter what she says, I know we both feel this connection.

What bothers me most is what Melanie said about Haylee thinking she is undeserving of love. Because *fuck*. What I wouldn't do to prove to her every goddamn day just how deserving she is.

I'm going over there first thing tomorrow to show her just how deserving she is, and as much as she wants to try, she's not pushing me away. I am more afraid of never giving what we have a shot than I am of her dickhead ex.

I'm sitting on Nik and Alyssa's deck, where I spend most every morning drinking my espresso and reading the paper. I want Haylee; how could I not? I crave this woman with every ounce of my soul. I already made a pot of coffee for Haylee, knowing she'll be down for it any time now.

I hear her delicate feet come down the stairs and clank around coffee cups, opening the fridge for her caramel coffee creamer. I watch as she wraps her delicate fingers around the mug, embracing the sunlight beaming through the kitchen window. A sunrise I admired only moments ago, but hell if I don't like this view better.

When she walks out onto the deck, she glares at me, taking

the seat next to me. Her hair is in a messy bun, her oversized shirt hanging off one shoulder, exposing her delicate skin. Skin my lips tasted only days ago. I smirk at the creases left behind on her cheek from her good night's sleep.

She looks good like this.

I wonder if this is what she'd look like after coming on my dick all night. Disheveled, glowing, and completely satiated. My eyes trail back to see her eyebrows drawn together. *Oh, she looks furious. Shit.*

"Rough night?" I question.

I need to tell her, to show her that I don't give a fuck about that piece of shit Paul. *I dare you, asshole . . . try touching her.* I'm here for her, no matter how many times she turns me down.

She gives me another death stare. "How was *your* night with your *lady* friend?"

Yup, I'm definitely in for it now. Shit. Shit. Shit.

She must've seen Melanie coming over. How the hell do I explain this one?

"Good." I turn to her with a devilish smile. "I thought I could fuck you out of my system, since you turned me down and all." We have been nothing but honest from the start. Why stop now?

She turned *me* down.

She told *me* she can't.

She has no right to be pissed, but hell am I happy that she is. It only further proves everything I thought I knew. The constant heat searing between us. It's undeniable.

"And did it work?" She looks at me, lifting one eyebrow.

"No. She didn't have a smart mouth like you, so she couldn't get my dick hard." She tries to mask her slight laugh and fails as she fixes her smile back into an adorable mask of displeasure.

We both know I hear it. With those few words, I made my point, so I head out for another long day of work.

NIK

Family night. Dinner's at 6.

KNOX

See ya there.

It's been two days since I indirectly told Haylee I didn't fuck Melanie. Haylee's been making it a point to not talk to me. I keep catching her eyeing me, but not a word. The same silence she's gifted me with for the past several days continues.

We have gotten into a routine after her confession of seeing me with Melanie, and my not so modest attempt of telling her I only had eyes for her. It starts at 5 a.m., with me making her a pot of coffee as I work on my espresso. We then sit side by side in comfortable silence, her reading one of Alyssa's books, and me with the paper.

More often than not, I'm staring at her, wondering what she's reading that could possibly make her eyebrows shoot up, a smile flash across her face, or my absolute favorite—the blush that flushes her cheeks. Every so often, she catches me watching her intently, her eyes melting with mine before giving me an irresistible smile followed by a scowl.

Tonight's game is charades. We've been playing for forty minutes and no one has guessed a thing right yet. Haylee is tossing her hands up in the middle of the room and running back and forth as if she's swimming.

The timer goes off. "Riptide! It was riptide!" Haylee yells, throwing her arms in the air, repeating the motion.

I catch Nik smirk at his wife. "We suck at this. How about Never Have I Ever."

I reach for my beer, adjusting myself closer to Haylee, and her cold foot brush against my thigh. She pulls back before giving me an apologetic look. She knows she can only be mad at me, hell, maybe even herself, for so long.

I place my hand on top of the blanket and hold her foot that's curled alongside her. Back and forth, I caress her foot to warm her, not hiding our interaction. A sense of relaxation overcomes me at the simple contact.

Haylee sits forward to adjust herself, my hand falling free from her, and I feel a loss at the contact. She positions her feet to her opposite side as I readjust my arm and place it on the back of the couch. To my surprise, she moves closer to me, nuzzling into my warmth, pulling the blanket across us. My hand finds her shoulder from the back of the couch, grazing the skin behind her ear as her head leans against my shoulder.

Alyssa notices and gives me an approving smile and nods when no one is looking. She knows our interactions to an extent. How much it means to me to find someone to share my life with and have a family of my own. I'm not exactly sure that's what this is, but I am certain it's worth finding out.

We go back and forth with several Never Have I Ever's. My hand never leaves the smooth skin of Haylee's neck. I can't help myself when I say, "Never have I ever puked on someone."

Haylee lets out a playful gasp and her eyes widen at me in horror.

About fuckin' time. Back to our normal song and dance.

She readjusts into my hold, taking another sip from her beer. "Never have I ever not been able to get my dick hard." Haylee looks at me with a victorious grin.

My hand halts on the back of her shoulder, and I give it a

tight squeeze. She lets out the softest moan only I can hear. My dick twitches at the sound.

I lean to her ear to whisper, "Not having that issue right now, honey." I give her a wink, tipping my beer toward her before it reaches my lips. I watch as the crimson red sneaks from her cheeks to the hem of her V-neck.

"My turn!" Alyssa shouts. She stands and eyes Nik. "Never have I ever been pregnant with a girl." Her eyes gleam at Nik. His eyes meet her in a standoff as he processes her words before he jumps up and hugs his wife. He lifts her up, hugging her, and then spins her around the room as they both shed tears of happiness. Haylee and I clap and shout in excitement over the news.

Wasting no time to treasure the moment with his wife, Nik smacks Alyssa's ass and scoops her up, carrying her up the stairs.

Nik shouts down to us, "Sorry to ditch! But we have more pressing matters!"

I'm glad he's happy. I know he wanted a boy. Someone to carry on his family name, to learn to shoot, to care for the farm. He deserves it. They both deserve all the happiness, but I can't help but feel a bit envious.

Haylee's quick to head into the kitchen, washing out the glasses from their virgin pina coladas. She looks so damn good standing there, wearing short pajamas shorts along with my hoodie. Her legs are tan and smooth, and her ass cheeks are just visible. I imagine what those legs would look like around my neck.

I stride toward her and wrap my hands around her from behind, taking the glass from her hand and placing it down into the sink. I press myself into her back, my dick hard again just from the sight of her.

The second moan of the night escapes her. I bury my smile

into her shoulder at the victory, placing a kiss on her skin. She's likely going to turn me down, but I have to touch her. My lips graze her ear and I try my best to whisper over my faint growl, "I have no problem getting hard for you."

Knox is making it so hard to not just ravish him. After our encounter on the deck, I had finally told Alyssa all the details of what happened. She was excited, to say the least. Planning double dates, rambling about moving and saying that our kids could grow up together. I definitely didn't miss the smirk she tossed Knox's way when he wrapped his arm around me.

I told her that right now it's nothing more than an attraction. Deep down, I know it's not true. There's more between us than sexual attraction. So much more. All my life, I just thought people were too emotional. The books, the movies, the couples with their never-ending Instagram posts. Now, though, I finally get it. I just had never seen or felt it. The sudden buzz that courses through my veins at just the mention of his name, the chest tightening nervousness that envelops me at the sight of him. I get it. I finally get it and it's a feeling I never want to lose.

I can't do this to him though, can I? As much as I want him, it will end horribly and I will drag him down with me. I am far from having my life figured out. I'm paying for an apartment in a city I don't live in and have a crazy stalker ex who will do god knows what. I come with so much baggage I just can't see how he would want to take on any of it.

Thinking of him in the truck, wiping away my tears, telling me he will keep me safe, singing like he's freakin' Luke Bryan, the way he plays back at my never-ending banter, the ease I find just being in his company. Alyssa used to say I was too much woman for Paul and that he didn't know how to fulfill my needs. In some way, maybe she was right.

Seeing Knox with another woman the other night, though, yeah, I was pissed. At first, I thought he wanted me to be jealous. And I was, but hearing him say he needed to get me out of his mind blew me away. He wasn't doing it to be vengeful. He was trying to heal himself.

Even if it was with his dick.

It takes much more to hurt my feelings. Try being with a narcissist who doesn't care about you. Lies and gaslights you every step of the way. Makes you out to be the toxic one. It gives you thicker skin. Knox put himself out there. He's the one who got walked away from. Yet, he's back, admitting he couldn't get it up for another woman. For whatever reason, that pleases me.

Good Lord, I want him. I do, I really fucking do. I don't want him hurt because of my fucked-up past, but what does that mean? That Paul is winning, yet again. Do I want to constantly live in fear of him and never be able to live my life?

I turn around to face Knox. "I just don't want you caught up in all this." I put my hands out to my sides as if I have all my baggage laid out on display for him. "What if . . . he finds out. That won't end well for either of us."

Knox grips the back of my neck, forcing me to turn my head toward him so my eyes connect with his. His hands are so large, they wrap around to my cheeks with a gentle stroke of his thumbs.

"Haylee, if it means I get to have all of you, then I want to be caught up in all of it." His voice is stern and sincere.

My chest flutters. *Have all of you.* I don't know what Paul will do, but I am certain, though, that if I miss my chance with Knox, I will live with that regret until the day I die.

I slowly give into the urge, faintly brushing my lips against Knox's. His scent, his words, his security. It's all too much to pass over in this moment. When my name passes through his lips, I succumb to him.

Our lips gently move together, but I can still feel every bit of Knox surrounding me. His hand cradles the base of my neck, his other at my waist, pulling me toward him. At the loss of his soft lips, his eyes trace over me instead. I know he is holding back the idea of tossing me over his shoulder and carrying me to his house.

I want it. I want all the roughness he's promised. I trust him. As much as this man can be feared, he would never harm me.

"You want to be caught up in it? Not just because I'm the only one who can get you hard?" I say. My brain and my vagina are clearly not on the same page.

I shouldn't be provoking him. But fuck. I want this just as bad as he does. I'm just afraid there will be consequences. Me, heartbroken if I fall for him or both of us, taking the brunt force of Paul.

He lets out a sigh that might as well be a growl. "I'm going to teach that dirty little mouth a lesson." A shiver of excitement runs through my entire body. Screw this. Screw Paul. He is not taking any more from me. I never wanted a man more than I want Knox right now.

I lean in, grazing his lips, and bite his bottom lip before stepping backward to the kitchen sink. "What are you going to do about it? Spank me?"

I turn my ass toward him, brushing over his hard cock. I

can't help but let out a slight giggle when he takes in a sharp breath. He slides his palm over my ass from under my shorts, tilting his head back and moaning as he grips onto me. With two hands, he quickly yanks down my pajama shorts, leaving me in nothing but my sweatshirt and thong. He gives my ass a quick, hard smack.

The wetness pooling between my legs surprises me. *Never* has a smack sent so much pleasure through my veins. Yet, I have never truly felt safe in the hands of another man. He caresses his palm over the sting and leans down to place his lips on the pink skin. It's a kiss I feel flutter to my core. Turning to face Knox, I place my hands on the counter behind me. The action lifts my sweatshirt and gives him a better view of my black lace thong.

Knox looks me over with a hunger in his eyes and lifts me up, so my bare ass is on the counter. His hands still gripping my hips, his lips land on my neck, and trace their way under my—well, his—sweatshirt.

"Let me see the rest of that outfit, honey." He takes a step back, as if he's resisting the urge to devour me right here.

I know Nik and Alyssa are busy upstairs and they never come back down after calling it a night. So, in one swift move, I pull my sweatshirt over my head. Exposing him to my matching lace bra. It's completely see through and my most comfortable, barely-wearing-a-bra bra.

Knox leans against the counter opposite me. One hand tightly gripping the counter, the other made into a fist, biting his knuckles behind a slight smirk.

"You know I have been wondering what you had on under there all night?" Knox's eyes roam over my entire body, as if this is the first time he has seen me naked. The first time both of us were coherent, maybe. His hand moves to play with the scruff on his chin as if he is deep in thought as to what to do with me. My heart pounds at the thought.

I run my hand over my bralette and down my stomach, toward my thigh to open my legs for him. "Having any issues getting it up now?"

"Honey, the thought of you even in sweatpants with spaghetti sauce on your shirt gets me hard. This, though, you, right now, naked and spread out on the counter for me like a fucking treat. Now that has me about to come in my jeans. Now open up and let me see how wet you are for me," he says, holding onto the counter behind him like if he lets go, he's going to tackle me.

I open my legs wider and slide my panties to the side. I slowly slide my finger down over my clit. I moan at the contact. Fuck, I could come just from him watching me like this.

"Now show me how you touch yourself when you think of me."

My cheeks heat at his words. Oh god, this man wasn't lying when he said he is the real thing. I run my free hand under the cup of my bra, freeing my breasts.

"Fuck, Haylee," he says as I pebble my nipple and continue to rub. "Good girl, now let me see your fingers in that perfect pussy," he demands. I slowly glide my finger inside myself, pulling in and out slightly. I need more. I need him. I want to feel him. I slide a second finger in and thrust it into myself harder. My eyes are locked to Knox's as his eyes memorize the moment, completely enamored. I need him to hurry up and touch me already. Moaning in pleasure, I feel my arousal dripping onto the counter.

"Knox, I need you."

Knox is to me before I finish my sentence, pulling my legs toward him, sliding my ass to the end of the countertop.

"I will punish that sweet little mouth of yours later. Right now I need to worship you."

He kisses my nipple, flicking it with his tongue. He runs

his tongue along my stomach and traces a hand down my inner thighs. My entire body is yearning in anticipation. He makes his way lower, lifting me up, and sliding my panties off in one easy motion as my sweaty palms grip the counter. Knox's mouth never leaves my skin, as he makes his way down to my sensitive clit. My every sense takes him in as he surrounds me, his strong voice, to his masculine scent, the taste of his mouth on my tongue, to the feel of his stubble rubbing my inner thigh. My head falls back in pleasure as my moans fill the room. He laps his tongue over my clit as he bends over the countertop, holding onto me with a tight grip.

Oh my god.

This man is a god.

It's as if he's on a mission to taste every drop of my arousal, his mouth sucking and licking, over and over, as his fingers curve into me. Surrounded by Knox's scent and the never ending dirty praise spewing from his lips, I am seconds away from coming.

"Fuck, Knox. Yes, don't stop," I plead, shuttering beneath him, and crying his name between moans.

"You taste so fuckin' good, Haylee. Come for me, honey."

My nails dig into his shoulders as I thrust my hips against his mouth, taking everything he's offering. My walls tighten around his fingers, reveling his touch. My body shutters as I tense and tremble beneath him.

I shiver as I come down from my orgasm. Every one of my senses heightened to pure euphoria. He kisses me back up my thigh, my stomach, and then his tongue flicks my nipple as I begin to catch my breath.

I have orgasmed many times, but nothing has ever compared to how this felt. I can only imagine what it feels like to have him inside of me. Holding me, he leans back, taking in the view of me, his beard glistening with my arousal. Knox kisses my lips, his forehead meeting mine with a deep exhale. "You are absolutely perfect for me."

I have to roll over to face the clock on my bedside table to see that it is 2 a.m. People usually sleep after a mind blowing orgasm, right? Not me, though. I can't stop going through all the what ifs. All my life I've felt like I've never been enough. My education, my job, my clothes were never enough for my parents. With Paul, he made sure to make me feel like I didn't deserve him. As if I was nothing without him.

With Knox, I feel every bit of myself. I'm not pretending to be someone I'm not. He likes me for who I am. Not the act I put on or the family I come from.

To him, I am enough.

He doesn't want to change me or use me like a puppet. The past few weeks of being with Knox, I've shown him more of myself than I ever have to my parents, coworkers, or to Paul.

I still am fearful of what's to come, even with Knox saying he'd happily take on my baggage. Knox thinks he knows, but he truly has no clue what he's signing up for.

What does he even want?

Is this a one-night stand? An occasional hook up while I'm around? A relationship? I haven't dated in years, and when I did, that was in college. I mean, we haven't even been on a date. Don't people date before shoving their tongue between someone's legs?

To top it all off, I don't even live in Texas, even though it's been on my mind for years to get out of New York. What happens when I go back home or when Paul shows back up? Will he still be around for that? The break-ins, the stalking, showing up at my work. There's no way a man like

Knox will stand for that with someone he cares for. Is this just fun to him? Did I just open up an entirely new can of worms?

His presence alone is a security I've never felt. The way he looks at me, the way I can be unexplainably myself, the way I don't feel like I have to put on this fucking fake smile just to appease someone else's feelings.

I can't put him in this situation.

I cannot fall for this man. For both our sakes. Two people can just hook up. No strings attached. Right?

ALYSSA

You dirty dirty girl

HAYLEE

What?! What did I do?

ALYSSA

My ring camera might have spotted you and a certain someone in the kitchen last night.

Oh my god.

I immediately press *call*, and before Alyssa gets a chance to answer, I'm deep in panic. "You have a camera in the kitchen?" I whisper shout into the phone.

Not that anyone can hear me. I'm on the porch reading, but you never know when someone might show up. This house is a revolving door of workers from the ranch.

"Yeah, Nik set them up. There's one in the kitchen, pointed near the entrance, and another on the driveway. Ya know, in case there's ever an intruder," she says it like it's no big deal, but her nonchalant tone immediately calms me.

"Erghm, did you watch it?!" The guilt of having Knox's head between my thighs on her countertop hits me full force. Of course she watched it, even though I'm sure not in its entirety. She called me a dirty girl. Jesus. I need to find a whole new family now.

"Well, no, but you know all of Nik's little gadgets. He has that screen in the bedroom, you know, the one I yell at to play my music, but never listens to me when I ask it to."

I let out a deep sigh in embarrassment. "Yesss." I can remember back to watching Alyssa yell at Alexa to play Usher fifteen times before calling it a *little bitch*. I can picture the driveway displayed on the screen, rolling my eyes at myself as I press my fingertips into my forehead.

"So, Nik got up to pee and saw you guys getting down to business before turning it off. I deleted it all. Don't worry. But I did send it to your email first. You're welcome."

I'm not surprised in the slightest. Alyssa's always been one to be open about anything sexual. I can picture her sitting on her bed, clapping in excitement, and making a comment to Nik about cobwebs or some crap.

I quickly put her on speakerphone, clicking open my email, opening the file from Alyssa. The subject line: Disinfect my counters.

I click play on the attachment. "Oh my god." I cover my mouth in embarrassment, watching Knox dip his head down, knowing exactly what's coming. Heat spreads over my cheeks and throughout my body.

I pause the video, bringing my attention back to my sister. "Are you sure that you deleted it, Lyss?" She laughs and I can hear her typing on her computer working. "Yes, I'm positive. You have the only copy. Gotta get back to work. See ya later, though?"

She's completely unfazed by the bomb she dropped on me.

"Yup. See ya later." I click end on the call and press play again on the video.

Holy shit.

I should just leave well enough alone; repercussions are sure to follow, but heat fills my stomach as I watch it. I download the video to my phone, saving it for a late night when it might come in handy. I then send it off to Knox in a text. You can't see much, just my exposed breasts. Knox's head covers all the good stuff. I look good and even though I'm not sure what me and Knox have, I can't find it in myself to get distance. I definitely don't see the harm in flirting. Well, I guess this might be justified as sexting?

Chapter Eighteen
Knox

Looking around my childhood home, I smile. It looks nothing like it did growing up, but still holds all its original charm. A family is going to love this place. When my parents passed away, it was all mine. Yet I haven't spent a single night here since before my first deployment. The house has held so much pain for me. This will always be where I was told my parents were dead. The place I hid alone and scared for so many nights. Before that, it was filled with laughter and happiness. My mom cooking waffles on a Sunday morning, my dad taking my mother by the hand and dancing her down the hallway. All memories scorched in one night. It's why I stay at the cabin at Nik and Lyss's, the painful memories blurring the good.

I scratch my head, taking in my soon to be Airbnb. I look around from the kitchen to the living room. The arched windows that reach the ceiling let in sunlight into the living room and the loft above. The white sectional wraps around in a U, pointing directly at the TV. A wooden coffee table sits underneath an iron sphere light that I paid way too damn much for. Kitchen appliances and a customer-made butcher's block line the marble counters. It all looks good, but there's still something missing.

I can't put my finger on it.

What is it?

I grab my phone from the back pocket of my jeans to text Haylee. She sent me a text a few hours ago with a video of our hook up. I couldn't help but be angry with myself for forgetting Nik set those cameras up. I am going to kick his ass if he watched it. Hell, I'm going to kick his ass just for knowing about it.

KNOX

Meet me at 32 Old Ridge Rd.

HAYLEE

Want to explain why?

KNOX

I need your womanly expertise.

HAYLEE

We aren't doing that again.

KNOX

You keep telling yourself that. But no that's not what I need your help with. Not yet at least.

I sit on the step of the front porch. Taking a much-needed break from the onslaught of shit on my to-do list. Hearing the noise of tires pulling up the gravel, I sip from my to-go mug, place it on the steps, and make my way to Haylee's driver's side door.

"Hey you," she says, stepping out of the car. She gives me a quick peck on my cheek as if I didn't just have my head between her legs last night.

Okay, so this is how it's going to be.

"I hope you weren't busy. I just really need your advice on some things."

"Of course, happy to help." Haylee turns back into the car with her ass sticking out of the driver's side door to grab her phone and wallet. She must've been working out. She's wearing a tight crop top that must double as a sports bra with the tightest pair of leggings and sneakers. I put my hands in my pockets as much-needed protection from me groping her like a high schooler.

"I had just gotten back from my run. It was perfect timing," she says, pulling herself out of the car to face me.

A smirk covers my face as I take her in. I've never seen her like this. Usually, she has make-up and her hair styled in waves down her back. Her hair is up in a high ponytail that reaches the middle of her back, and not a trace of makeup on.

She's fucking stunning.

"What?" She raises an eyebrow at me, surely wondering what I'm thinking as I eye fuck the shit out of her.

I close the space between us. She backs up into the car as I remove my hands from the restraint of my pockets. I need to touch her now that I've had a taste of her.

I place my hand on the side of her neck, up the back of her head as I lean in. My hand moves to her ponytail and I twirl it through my fingers before fisting it. She takes in a sharp inhale.

"I like this." I lightly tug on her ponytail now wrapped around my hand. The exposed skin on her neck calls to me and I kiss it, my lips lingering against her beating pulse. "Something for me to hold onto while you're on your knees with your mouth around my dick," I whisper.

The image of her on her knees invades me. Her bright red nail polished fingers wrapped around my length. Her moans vibrating around my cock. Brown tear-filled eyes looking up to me in adoration. I feel the twitch in my jeans and her heavy slow breaths on my ear. I tear myself away from the fantasy.

Her cheeks flush as she giggles at my comment. Slowly, I line kisses up Haylee's neck, taking in her sweet scent, making my way to her full lips as mine connect with hers. She's irresistible. Even feeling her smile against my mouth sends me for a loop. I nibble her bottom lip and it takes everything in me to pull away, knowing I have work to do inside. This is how she deserves to be greeted, not pecks on the cheek.

I give Haylee a bit of insight on my plan to use my childhood home as a rental as we make our way inside. We move around the house, going room to room, as I explain how I can't seem to pinpoint exactly what's missing.

"I can picture it," Haylee says as she runs her fingers along the kitchen countertop. "You with your backpack, eating cereal and running to the bus. Doing homework while your mom makes dinner." She looks up at me to meet my eyes with a smile.

I can't remember the last time someone mentioned my mother with such ease. It's always been a topic most people tread far away from, unknowing how I'd react. I smile, thinking of all the mornings before school, the smell wafting through the house. "Waffles, actually. She made me waffles just about every day."

Haylee's face lights up, looking at the barstool at the kitchen island. I can tell she's picturing a younger, less fucked up version of me, babbling on to my mom, scarfing down my breakfast. Hell, I'm picturing it too.

"Why don't you live here?" Her expression falls, and she opens the empty fridge, searching through it as if something will appear.

"It just hasn't felt like home in a long time." I grab my keys from the counter and check for my wallet in my back pocket. "Since the night I was told they passed, it just never felt the same again." She takes in my words and looks around the space. Haylee grabs an old invoice off the counter, flipping it over before beginning to write.

Haylee explains it's missing the cozy home vibe, whatever that means. That I need pillows, blankets, plants, and candles. I'm not sure if that's the solution to my problem, but watching her tap the pen against her lips as she talks has me entranced. Plus, I'm sure as hell not going to pass up spending more time with her. Even if that means her spending an obscene amount of money decorating a home I'll never live in.

"Well, then. Let's add a little love back in it."

Her whole expression brightens, and her eyes glisten with joy.

I'm going to spend so much fucking money.

We drive an hour to Target, and Haylee fills two carts until they are overflowing. I'm pretty sure whoever Chip and Joanna Gains are, we own just about everything they sell. *We.* When did I start labeling my things as hers? I like that.

We.

Ours.

It's almost two in the morning and we have been up all night strategically placing potted plants, books, toothbrush holders. It's been an exhausting day. I can barely pull myself up from leaning on the counter. I watch Haylee fold and unfold a blanket several times, draping it over the back of the couch that's now filled with oversized pillows and several other blankets. The space looks lived in, bright . . . happy even.

Haylee grabs the blanket back off the couch a third time. She flings it over her shoulders and pulls it around her. She looks tired too, but her face is full of happiness and warmth. I can't pull my eyes away from her.

All night she's been bouncing around decorating while dancing and singing to her playlist on the sound system, her scent now in every room. Takeout litters the counters and wine glasses sit on the coffee table. She's brought life back into this house. The laughs, giggles, and chatter that have been missing for so long.

I'm sure the shopping spree had something to do with it, but she was right. The house needed love. With her here, it's starting to feel like a home. I make my way over to the couch beside Haylee, who is bundled up in a new blanket. I pick her feet up and place them in my lap, rubbing the cold from them. They're always cold. I make a mental note to get her slippers if she's going to keep coming here since the tile floor is always cold.

Her exhausted body curls into me and her hand laces our fingers. It feels like the most natural thing. The entire world around me relaxes. Somehow, holding her in my arms releases all the stress I've been carrying from my parents' accident and all the shit I've seen on tour. I revel in the peace she brings me.

Her eyes are heavy as she blinks slowly. "Did we do it? Did we fix what was missing?" I squeeze her hand and place a kiss on top of her head.

I pause, looking around the room and back down to her. "Yeah, honey, I found what was missing." Her eyes close and I can tell she's fallen asleep. I place another kiss gently on her head. My eyes close as thoughts of what a future would look like with Haylee consumes me. I am certain I'm falling for this woman.

Chapter Nineteen
Haylee

I cannot say that I've ever been happier than I am right now. My one-way ticket has brought me to almost spending a month on the ranch. Alyssa and I have always shared a close bond, having basically just each other as family to lean on. She read me bedtime stories, and I helped her with her algebra. We were two peas in a pod.

Like with any adulthood, we eventually drifted apart. We have never gone without speaking on the phone and texts throughout the day, but having the ability to run to her room and tell my secrets again, and staying up late playing board games, is just something I didn't realize our relationship was missing.

Last weekend Alyssa, Annabeth, and a few of their closest friends let me tag along for a girls' night out. I haven't been out with girlfriends in years—not since college at least, and definitely not while I was with Paul.

I always had to come home right after work. I could only have a girls' night at home with friends he approved of. It was mainly new friends that he knew would never dig too deep into our lives by asking too many questions.

Annabeth and I immediately hit it off, singing karaoke and, embarrassingly enough, dancing on the bartop. Who knew she had it in her?

Hell, who knew I had it in me?

I will absolutely be avoiding that bar for several weeks. I was surprised Annabeth even remembered my bucket list, let alone things that were on it.

The day after, I woke up to a massive hangover and a text from Annabeth to meet at a bench in the town center. She brought coffees and donuts, having explained the donuts will absorb the alcohol, essentially curing the hangover. Nothing like the frenzy of a woman I had gotten to know the night before.

I sort of envy who she is—professional and charming, with a bit of a wild, carefree side. Since our picnic, we've met up several more times. Looking at her now, I am glad to know I have a genuine friend here.

I sip the coffee she brought from the shop. "I should really start paying for these."

"Oh please, Haylee. It's like fourteen espresso beans and a paper cup. We are friends. You don't owe me a thing."

"Thank you, I really appreciate that. But next time, I'm buying the donuts then." I pick up a donut and cheers my strawberry frosted to her glazed donut in agreement.

Giggling at our exchange, I see Knox striding our way. My heart flutters and I can't help but lock eyes with him. We have seen each other just about every day since I've been in Canyon Falls, but we have done nothing but make out like teenagers. Even though I know Knox is just as eager as I am to take it further.

He hits me with the most charming grin accompanied by his signature panty-melting wink and head nod.

He stops, his wide frame towering over us on the bench. "Haylee. AB."

Annabeth is not unfamiliar with our situation and holds a donut out toward Knox. "Hi Knox, donut?"

Knox's eyes stay glued to mine, never straying back to Annabeth after his curt hello. "No, thank you, Annabeth. I'm having my dessert later, after the big game." With that, he takes his finger and swipes at the remnants of strawberry frosting from the corner of my lip. I'm too taken off guard to be embarrassed when he then takes his finger to his mouth, sucking the frosting away. "And it's going to be delicious."

With another wink, Knox makes his way in the opposite direction as Annabeth fans herself.

"Good grief, woman. I think he would've taken you right here if wasn't sitting next to you."

"I somehow don't even think you're wrong. Would you even judge me if I let him?"

She laughs, popping the last bite of her donut into her mouth. "So I went into the library the other day and Marcie, the librarian, was telling me about how you paid for Cade Fullers' college application."

She sits on her words, waiting for me to respond. "Yeah. I did. He needed help and I could help him. It wasn't really a big deal, ya know."

"That is a big deal, Haylee. No one else I know would front the money for someone else's kid's college application. Marcie said you were great with him and now she's getting asked by other parents if they offer college prep classes."

"Really, it was no big deal. I just felt for him. No kid should struggle with something like applying for college. It can determine their entire future. I'd hate to see a kid not have a chance to apply just because they can't afford an application fee or they're struggling to write an essay."

"Well, Marcie didn't think it was no big deal. She

mentioned to me how she thought it would be a great idea to have a program like that for the kids in town. She wanted to know if you'd be interested in helping her out with arranging something for them."

I am shocked. I didn't realize anyone around could hear me and Cade. It would be a huge success for this town to have such a program. It would take stress off the kids and, hell, even help me find a purpose other than my current unfulfilling career.

Maybe I could pitch some of my other ideas to financially help kids like Cade. "Of course, I would want to be a part of that, Annabeth. That sounds incredible! You let her know I would do it, right?"

"Well, no, I wanted to mention it to you first, of course."

"Well, tell her yes! Of course!"

It catches me off guard to see Paul's message. Between falling for Knox and not having the constant bombarding messages from Paul, I feel like I've been living in a bubble. But it was only a matter of time before Paul found a new way to contact me.

I am without a doubt falling for Knox and I am doing nothing but putting him in harm's way. After seeing him in his childhood home, my heart broke for the little boy he once was. He was eighteen years old, all alone in a house with no one to rely on but himself.

How does anyone go through what he did, see the things he's seen, and turn out to be so kind, compassionate, and tender? I want to latch onto him. Hold him while telling him everything will be okay. I want to spend my life wrapped in his arms where I know I'm safe from the evils of this world.

But I can't.

I can't jeopardize the safety of everyone I've ever cared about, even if it means losing him.

"You sure you can't stay longer? The boys have a game tonight," Alyssa says as she neatly folds a pile of laundry from my hamper. She says it's relaxing and part of the nesting process.

"I really need to get back to my life, Lyss. I've already been here longer than I even planned," I lie, having nothing to go back to. I'm going to miss seeing her every day. Watching that bump grow.

"Then why does it feel like you're leaving so abruptly? Did something happen?"

"Nothing happened. I just can't stay here anymore. It's all too much." My words come out broken, holding back tears.

She stops folding my mound of laundry and pulls me to sit on the bed, bringing me in for a hug. My tears begin to fall the second my cheek presses to her shoulder.

"I'm scared. I'm scared he will hurt someone I care about." My words are muffled into her sweater. "I don't know what I'd do if he showed up and hurt one of you. It'd be all my fault, Lyss. He said he's coming for me and I know he means it." The thought of my sister, the baby, or Knox being hurt sends chills down my spine and draws a primal feeling from my chest.

The thought of leaving breaks my heart even more.

Alyssa grabs me by the shoulders and pulls me away from

her, looking into my eyes. "Hay, I have never seen you happier than in the last few months here. If you want to leave, I will drive you to the airport right now. But I don't want you to leave because you think it's what's best for the rest of us. Secondly, the decisions Paul makes are on *him* and *him* only. The consequences for *his* actions are not your responsibility to bear. You need to make this decision for you and only you. Not for me or this baby or for Knox. Not out of fear of what may or may not happen. What do you want? What makes you happy?"

Chapter Twenty
Knox

"What's got you so happy?" Nik asks as I sip my coffee, eyeing the spot on the counter me and Haylee once occupied.

"Nothing, just excited for our game," I fib, glancing back to the counter.

"I'm going to load up the truck. Can you get the girls?" he says, grabbing his catcher's gear on his way out the door.

I take a few more sips of coffee and go to the sink to wash my mug. I can't think of the last time I've been this happy. I'm smiling at a goddamn coffee mug. The hold this woman has on me, though, I've never felt anything like it. Everything with Haylee has just fallen into place. I've wanted the wife and family, but I never expected to want her in my childhood home, yet all I can imagine is her being there with me every day for the rest of our lives. I even question if I should start moving myself back into the house. I never anticipated the anger and resentment I've held on to for over a decade to subside, but with Haylee, it melts away.

I dry my mug and place it back on the counter before

making my way upstairs to find the girls. "Bus is leaving," I shout, turning into Haylee's room.

My smile comes crashing down when I catch sight of Haylee's tear-soaked face over Alyssa's shoulder. "What happened?" I say, standing at the door.

My eyes catch sight of the suitcase on the floor and the already packed bag on the bed.

She's leaving.

She can't leave. This just started. My stomach sinks and my throat immediately tightens. I can't imagine her not here in Canyon Falls, not here with me.

Haylee's eyes meet with mine and Alyssa catches sight of me. "I'll see you in a bit, Hay," Alyssa says, walking out the door and shutting it behind her.

I immediately make my way to the bed where Haylee is and place my hands on her face, wiping away the tears.

"Haylee, honey, what happened?" I glance around the room once again, confirming her packed bags. "You're leaving?"

The last time I saw her, she was giggling as I lined kisses up her neck after another game night, then quickly again when she was with Annabeth.

What happened in such a short time? She grips my forearms as I continue to look into her eyes. "I've lived the last decade making decisions based on Paul's actions. Will he raise his voice because I overcooked the chicken? Will he hit me because I was late leaving work? Will he accuse me of cheating on him?" She lets out a strangled laugh as another tear falls down her face. "Will he force himself on me while I'm asleep, or will he drink just enough to not be able to make it to bed? I don't know why I didn't see it until now. I thought when I left, I'd be free of him, but that will just never be the case."

I lean back on the pillow, closing my eyes as the silence

grows heavy between us. I hold her hand tightly as I try to picture my life without her here.

She's leaving.

She's leaving because some dirtbag didn't appreciate how fucking perfect she is.

God, I can't lose her.

Of course, I fall in love with the girl I can't have.

This girl that's so far out of my league. I let out a laugh at the thought of how pathetic I've come to be. I knew I wanted the house, the wife, and babies running wild, but god, what was I thinking? Of course, this girl doesn't want me. Why did I think she'd stick around? I feel her head lay on the pillow beside me.

"Haylee, I know I will never fully understand what it is you have had to endure with Paul. But what I do know is that he made you feel like you weren't enough, like the way he treated you was somehow your fault. But it wasn't, it never was. You deserve to be loved without fear. I know you won't go running back into his arms, but I am begging you to not run back to the hell you barely escaped from. Whatever you decide, I want you to know I see you for the strong, brave woman who survived what tried to break you. You don't need saving, and I am not trying to tell you what to do, but I want you to remember you are allowed to be happy and I don't think leaving will make you feel how I know you feel here."

"No, I'm not leaving," she says, her response almost a whisper.

I open my eyes to see her smiling at me, her eyes wide and glassy. She traces the tattoo up my forearm, deep in thought.

"I'm staying. I'm staying because for the first time, I'm doing what I want. I can't live in fear of what Paul may or may not do. I deserve to be happy. I know there might be consequences, but I can't make decisions based on Paul anymore."

I let out the breath I've been holding in since the second I saw her packed bags and roll to face her.

"I know he made you think you deserved what he did to you, but I need you to know that's just not the case. You're so fucking perfect, Haylee. He's an idiot for not treating you the way you deserve—like a goddamn queen, Haylee. But you can't do that to me again. I thought for a second I was losing you and I can't lose you. When I told you I want all of you, I meant that."

She smiles knowingly and places a kiss on my arm. "Lucky for you, I'm sick and tired of playing the role of his happy little wife."

His fuckin' wife? Over my dead body. I quickly roll myself, pinning her arms above her head, and straddle her. We have been taking it brutally slow after our encounter in the kitchen, keeping it very PG-13. "Mention being his wife again, honey, and I'll be sure to tie you up just like this while I go get you a ring you deserve to wear." Her eyes go wide and I watch as all the blood rushes to her cheeks.

"And what makes you so sure I'll wear it?"

I let out a feral growl and I rest just enough weight so my dick presses against her. I lean over to whisper in her ear, kissing her lips at every pause. "Because you and I both know *I* will be the one putting a ring on your finger. That I will be the one kissing that bratty mouth at the altar. I will be the one your children call *Dad*."

Our kiss starts slow and passionate, then begins to move faster. I want to be with her—in her life, her memories, her future. But more than anything, at this very moment, I want to be inside her.

I can't help but take her in as her eyes cut through me. Her breath becomes heavy, and in my quick movement of pulling myself into her, her tank top shifts, letting her breast peek out. I lean down again and suck it into my mouth. She releases a moan as I trail more kisses along her neck and down her chest. Her hips lift into me, trying to find the pleasure we both are so desperate for. I make my way from her perfect pebbled nipples back to her neck and to her mouth. I'm taking pleasure in all she has to offer.

"Knox, I need you." Haylee pants before releasing another moan.

"Honey, I don't have a condom. I was expecting to go to a baseball game." I let out a defeated breath as she runs her hands inside my gym shorts and frees my dick from my boxers. I love that she isn't the least bit shy asking for what she wants.

"Knox, I don't care. I need you inside of me." I may have come several times at just the thought of her touching me, but her hand stroking my dick, begging me to fuck her, has me considering fucking her bare.

I know how badly she needs me inside of her. To feel that closeness and release the tension that's been built up for weeks. To release all the pain and smother her with all the love and affection she deserves.

She runs her fist up and down my length, and I pump my hips into her touch. My lips come to meet hers again, my tongue exploring her mouth.

In one quick motion, she takes control, her legs wrapping around me to roll us so I'm now beneath her, her legs straddling tightly around my hips. My length presses against her as she rocks into me, grinding onto me. Her eyes meet mine and she lifts her tank top over her head. I let out a groan, seeing her brown hair fall around her perfect breasts.

"Haylee, you're so damn beautiful." She pulls her shorts to the side with one hand and runs my dick against her slit. "Mmm, Knox," she moans. My god she's soaked for me.

She sits up to stand; the loss of her has me pulling my shorts down and jerking off at the sight of her stripping off her shorts. When she comes back down to straddle me, my hands caress over her curves, down to her ass.

"Haylee, are you on birth control?" Jesus, why am I being so difficult? I just need to be inside of her. I have never not used protection with a woman before, never having been with someone I fully trusted.

She runs the tip of my dick against her clit, her head falling back with pleasure. "No." Her response is breathy and full of need. "No, Knox. I'm not," she repeats.

God, she's fucking beautiful. I admire her perfectly pink peaked nipples. She leans her chest against mine as she rubs against my length. The room fills with moans of both pleasure and torture as she grinds against me. My free hand runs circles on her clit.

Fuck. I fucking need her.

"Fuck it. I need to be inside of you right now." My demand comes out harsher than I'd like. She shifts upward and lines herself up, slowly taking me inside her. She lets out another moan, lifting as she lowers herself to take a bit more of me. I revel in the feel of her as I watch her repeat the process, her arousal coating my dick over and over. It's mesmerizing.

"Good girl, you look so fuckin' perfect with my dick inside of you." I tilt my head back down to the bed, taking in the feel of not wearing a condom for the first time as I release a deep breath.

It's as if in my entire adulthood I never truly experienced sex. I can't help but buck my hips upward, the entire length of my dick inside her.

Haylee takes in a sharp inhale at the intrusion. I take her nipple in my mouth, sucking and nipping before returning the same gratitude to the other. She rocks faster against me, her fingers digging into my arms as I grip her ass. My eyes drink her in at the sight of her above me, wild and absolutely breathtaking.

She's about to come; I can feel the walls of her pussy tensing around me, which normally wouldn't be an issue. With this beautiful woman riding my dick like her life depends on it, I won't be able to pull out of her quick enough. I'm not sure if she forgot, or it just hasn't crossed her mind, but I need to say something.

"Honey, you need to slow down." I let out another moan. "God, you're so tight. If you come, I won't be able to hold back."

She doesn't slow her pace as our lips meet, mine trailing down her neck. "Yes, Knox, fuck, you're so deep—you feel so good."

I take in the feel of her around me, the look on her face as she moans my name in pleasure. She begins pushing her hips into me quicker, looking for release.

"I need more, Knox. Please." She's so polite when I'm fucking her.

"Fuck, honey, keep moving like that and I'm going to come in you." I can feel the tingle beginning to rise. God, I want to feel her come all over my dick, but fuck, why didn't I have a condom on me?

"I want to feel you come inside me." Her eyes are heated with desire and I don't even know if she realizes the words left her mouth.

My body takes over at her response and all I can think of is the feel of her slick, tight pussy suffocating my dick. All logical thinking goes out the window. I need this. I need to feel her come around me. I thrust upward as my hands grip her waist, slamming her into me over and over as pleasure begins to overcome us both. Every thrust deeper and deeper with our hungry rhythm.

"Please don't stop. I'm going to come."

"Look at me . . . that's it. Be my good girl and come all over me."

The hunger in her gaze has me exploding as I thrust into her. She shutters as she rides me and I release in her. Her pussy clenching around me, drawing out every drop of come as I continue to thrust into her.

Slowly moving in and out of her, I feel my come coat the inside of her. I just fucking came inside her. What the actual fuck did I just do? As she lifts off me, I watch, mesmerized, at the sight of my come dripping out from her pussy as she rolls to lie beside me. I gently kiss her lips, then her forehead.

Something primal comes over me and I trail kisses down her stomach. I glide my fingers through the mixture of her arousal and my come, as I leave a kiss to her pelvic bone.

"You look fuckin' incredible, honey, with my come dripping from your pussy like this." I flick my tongue against her clit and another shiver overcomes her; her sensations heightened.

I smile and lean in to kiss her again, pulling her into my arms, where she's meant to be. She kisses me softly and her eyes light up in shock as if she just realized what we did. "I can't believe I just let you come inside of me."

I let out a laugh like I hadn't painfully mentioned that. "That was a first for me and my god, it was nothing like I've ever experienced." I've fucked plenty, but never have I made love to a woman like that before.

"What if?" she hesitates, taking in what we really just did. Knowing what's at the tip of her tongue, I interrupt her.

"Honey, you're already mine and I love you. If this moment between us ends with you being pregnant with my child, then I am fucking over the moon about it."

Her eyes search my face, taking in the fact that I love her. Shit, I did just say that, didn't I? *I love her.* I know, without a doubt in my mind, that this woman will be my wife and the mother of my children. Maybe in nine months, maybe years from now. I'm certain of it, and I have not a single ounce of remorse for what we just did. Her lips find mine, showing me every ounce of appreciation to my words.

"I love you too, Knox." My chest constricts. I take my time appreciating her laying in my arms. I run my fingers through her hair as I kiss her, admiring her every feature.

"Can you wait and drive me to your baseball game once I shower?"

The game.

Shit, I completely forgot. I was grabbing the girls to head to the game. I lean over the bed and grab my phone from my shorts on the floor. We have fifteen minutes to get there. Not that I really care if I miss the game. I'm right where I need to be, but it's an important one and I'll be sure to spoil her more later.

"Game starts in fifteen minutes. You're going like that!" I jump from the bed and point at her. She's completely naked and shooting me a pissed off look as if it's my fault she won't have time to shower. Honestly, I'm happy she won't have time. She will be sitting watching my game, with my come dripping into her panties.

Just the thought has my dick hard again. I'm not surprised this woman helped me find a new kink. I make my way back to her, planting a kiss on her shoulder as she pulls her black panties back on. Her eyes catch the massive hard-on under my gray shorts.

"Really?" she says, her eyes glancing from my dick, then back up to me. I trace my hand down her bare back, to the black lace, sliding my hand around to the front and down to her slit, still soaked with my come. I moan as I swipe through her folds.

"It's the thought of my come dripping from your sweet, tight pussy, soaking through these black panties. It's driving me crazy." I tear my hand away, and the lace snaps against her. I know if I keep going, we will never leave this room.

I'm sitting next to Alyssa in our folding camping chairs, watching the boys play in their beer league. After the mind-shattering orgasm, Knox and I pulled up right in time for the game to start.

Nik just hit a grounder to left field making the bases loaded. Now, having watched a few games, I know that with Knox up to bat, the pressure's on. He hits homers pretty often, and a grand slam will make this game a for sure win.

"So, you had sex after you told him you were staying?" Alyssa asks, her eyes shifting back and forth between Nik and Knox on the field, the back on me. "Then proceeded to tell him to put a baby in you?"

Oh my god. I still can't believe we did that. I glance around to see who might have heard her.

It just felt so right. Even after talking to Alyssa, I didn't have a single doubt in my mind that I wasn't exactly where I was supposed to be. The city was always home for me. A giant city where I'd spent all my life. A city that *used* to give me a sense of comfort and security. Now, I want to be anywhere but home. Now I know with certainty, Alyssa, Nik, Knox, and my sweet unborn nephew are my home.

I glance toward Knox, who's waiting on just the right pitch. "Let's go, Knox!"

"It wasn't like that," I laugh. "We were in the heat of the moment. It was passionate and intense. It just finally felt right. Is it weird that we only met weeks ago, and it's possible I just let him get me pregnant?" The thought of Knox moaning my name at his release crosses my mind, and I clench my thighs at the image of him. "Maybe if you had some condoms in your house . . . " I huff.

"I'm pregnant, Haylee. What the hell would I need a condom for?"

I let out another laugh. If this situation occurred while I was with Paul, I would be panicked with anxiety. I would be out buying the day after pill. With Knox, I don't have a single drop of regret. I can't stop smiling. I've never been so certain that I was exactly where I was supposed to be; surrounded by people I love, in a town that I love.

From the outside, it might not make sense to everyone. But in the short time I've known Knox, I've shared more intimate and heartfelt conversations with him than I'd ever had with Paul.

Knox's bat connects with the ball. It flies right over the fence, clearing it by at least 5 feet. Alyssa and I jump to our feet, cheering and yelling as the boys run to home plate. Once Knox rounds the base, he winks at me.

The second I realize he's headed toward me, pulling his helmet off, I throw my empty soda can onto my chair and run into his arms. Giddy with excitement, my legs wrap around him, and he holds me with his hands planted on my ass. Neither of us caring who sees. Our lips immediately connect and I grip my hands behind his ears, pulling him into me, deepening our kiss.

Definitely need those.

I shake my head, silently laughing, picking up the box of condoms from the aisle in the local pharmacy and throwing them in my basket. Knox planned a date for us tonight and I could tell by the look in his eyes after his game yesterday that I better come prepared this time. I couldn't be more excited. Alyssa nudges my arm and lifts her brow.

"I'm happy for you."

I smile, because I'm happy for me, too.

I hear the bell on the door ring, alerting a customer walking inside the pharmacy, and the hairs on my neck stand up. My throat tightens and my stomach turns.

He's here.

I don't even have to see that Paul walked into the pharmacy to know that he's here.

He's here for me.

I peek past the aisle to confirm what my body already knows. Disheveled hair, unbuttoned shirt, and glassy eyes from god knows how much he's had to drink today.

I set down my basket and pull my phone from my back pocket. I open up my text thread with Knox. I won't have time to tell him what's happening, but I trust he will figure it out. I know when I hit share my location he will get an alert.

He will just know.

Just like my body knew Paul was here. Locking my phone and silencing it, I shove it into my cowgirl boot.

"Lyss, I'm just going to check out some of the makeup," I say, slowing my breathing and pointing to the front of the store. There's no way in hell I'm allowing anyone to put my sister or future nephew in harm's way.

I make my way to the registers and place my full basket on the counter. "Won't be needing this, thank you, sir. So sorry."

Paul's watching my every move. He knows Alyssa and I came together. He may be drunk, but he's still a detective and there's very little he doesn't see.

I keep my eyes forward, walking out of the pharmacy to put space between me and my sister. *He's here for me, not her*, I remind myself.

The bell chimes behind me as I suck in a deep breath, my heart pounding in my ears.

I turn the corner of the building, coming to a stop, and turn to face Paul. I think I could puke right here and now.

Paul raises his hand to my face, running his knuckles along my cheek. "I found you, baby."

I look down at the ground as his touch sends a cold chill down my spine. I breathe in deep to hold back the tears that are building. I just need to keep him calm.

He's clearly drunk, which means I have to choose my words wisely. "I've been right here," I say with a shrug, hoping to play it off like everything's just freaking peachy.

"Get in, I have something for you," he says, taking my purse and gripping me by the back of my arm. He motions me to his car, pushing my head down with force before slamming the door shut.

Chapter Twenty-Two
Knox

I finished my work on the ranch for the night and I have a couple of hours before my date with Haylee. I know we have done some things backward, but I want to make sure she gets everything she deserves. I can't wait to show her what I have planned. I pull a water bottle from the fridge, hearing a ding that I have a text. I grab my phone from my back pocket and laugh when I realize how giddy I am at the chance that Haylee texted me. I open my phone and my expression instantly falls.

TIME SENSITIVE

Haylee Hamilton started sharing their location with you.

I stare at the words on my screen, my heartbeat pounding in my chest. *Something's wrong.* She wouldn't just randomly start sharing her location with me for no reason unless there was a problem. She's supposed to be spending the day with Alyssa.

I click *call*, putting the phone up to my ear, and holding it with my shoulder as I unlock the safe in my bedroom. Every ring makes my pulse speed up as I think of all the reasons why. The call goes to voicemail and this time I call again, placing it on speaker beside me as I pull out my gun from the safe. I shove a magazine into my back pocket and click another into the gun. I get her voicemail twice more.

"Fuck, Fuck, Fuck."

I end the call and shoot her a text. I could be overreacting, but I have that gut fucking feeling that I'm not.

KNOX

I'm coming. I've got you.

I jump into my truck and immediately call Nik while flying down the driveway. I take a deep breath, attempting to calm myself while it rings. I've had the best training for the most intense scenarios. *I've got this.* But it's Haylee. *My Haylee.* I don't know what I'd do if anything happened to another person I loved. I hear Nik answer and don't let him get a word out.

"Haylee shared her location with me. Something's not right, Nik." I look both ways, yielding to the four-way stop in the road before blowing through it.

"Fuck. Where does it say she is? She's supposed to be with Alyssa. They were just at the pharmacy. I'm going to add her to the call. Hold on, buddy."

We all knew this was a possibility, but I just can't wrap my head around the fact that it's actually happening. Pulling into town, I park in front of the pharmacy and pull up the app tracking her location through town. I have no idea what I'm walking into.

Nik adds Alyssa to the three-way call. "Baby, it's okay. We

are going to find her. Tell Knox what you just told me." I can hear her crying and it immediately makes it feel like someone has their hand wrapped tight around my throat.

"She . . . she said she was going to look for makeup. I went to find her and the clerk said . . . he said that she left."

I can hear Nik on the line ruffling around and starting his car, leaving wherever he is. "What else, baby," Nik says.

"She left her basket of condoms without paying and I saw Paul outside the window, shoving her into a car. By the time I ran outside, they were gone."

I slam my fist into the steering wheel. "FUCK. How long ago?"

"About ten minutes. Seeing Paul stirred up my morning sickness. I didn't get a chance to call anyone right away, and now we've been on the phone for . . . ehh . . . three minutes?" she says, shame coating her every word. I look down at my call timer with Nik agreeing on the timeline. She hasn't been with Paul long and they're luckily not far away, but every second is one too long for me.

"I'll be there in thirty seconds," Nik says.

Haylee knew Paul was there before Alyssa even knew. I know she would do anything to keep her sister safe. Alyssa walks out the pharmacy door right as Nik pulls up behind my truck. He jumps out of the car, exchanging a few quick words with his wife, before jumping into my truck.

"Where to?" he asks, his eyes showing every ounce of fear I feel. Pulling out onto the road, I toss him my phone to watch her movement on the app.

"They look like they stopped just outside of town," I reply. The app doesn't show much; just a cutout of buildings and roads.

Nik pulls out his cell, his fingers moving over the keys almost as quickly as I'm driving. He's probably texting Alyssa, who was waiting on the local police department to take her statement.

"You're not going to like this."

"What now?" I growl, gritting my teeth.

"They're getting on the freeway." This fucker. He knows he can't force someone to get on a plane without drawing attention to himself. Does he really think he can just drive her back to New York and what? Pretend like nothing ever happened? My mind plays through all the possible scenarios as I press my foot harder on the pedal. He better not put a single fucking scratch on her.

Chapter Twenty-Three
Haylee

I stay silent, looking down at the liquor bottles at my feet, trying to steady my breathing. He thinks he's going to act like everything's normal and we'll go on a cruise or he'll buy me some new Hermes bag with a credit card I pay.

Nope. Not this time, asshole.

He cuts off another car who honks at him, and I grip the door. "I know you think I'm mad, baby, but we can fix this. You made a mistake. I forgive you, but it's time to come back home," he says, slurring his words.

Silence falls between us as I try to figure out how I'm going to get myself out of this. Do I tell him no? Do I apologize? Do I just go back to him to keep the people I care about safe?

"You know I hate being home without you. You know I still can't figure out that coffee machine."

What? Still can't? Has he been? No. He couldn't. There's no way he would have moved himself back into my apartment. I kicked him out.

"You've been back to the apartment?" I say, trying to act as casual as possible.

"Of course," he says as he leans forward toward the steering wheel, trying to get a better view of the road from his impaired vision. My eyes catch the familiar metal of a gun peeking out from the back of his jeans. My mouth dries and my stomach somersaults. I see the sign for the highway as we speed down the road.

Think, Haylee, think. I need a game plan. I've thought through every scenario of him showing up, but never thought it would be me willingly getting into a car with him. I look down at my phone lighting up in my boot. It's getting dark and if he sees it, he will know something's off. It's lighting up about every thirty seconds. Which means Knox got my message or Alyssa's wondering where I am.

I cross my ankles, hoping to cover the glow, praying Knox is tracking my every move. Paul reaches into the glove compartment, fumbling to pull out a bottle of whiskey.

"Oh yeah," he says, pulling out what looks like a travel bag. He fumbles some more, trying to hand me the bag while holding tight to the wheel, honking at the traffic as we invade their lane.

"Open it, baby."

Ugh, if he calls me baby one more time, I might just jump right out of the car.

I pull the velvet box from the bag, knowing it holds the same ring he had scoured my apartment for. I open the box to see the diamond glisten before me.

At one point, I had wished for this. For the ring, the wedding, the family. I had wanted this for so long, but so different from how I do now with Knox.

I pick it up and hold it out in front of me. "A ring," I say, not sure how to respond.

"Put it on."

I've thought of all the ways I'd be proposed to. Will it be romantic with candle light? Funny with a flash mob? Will my family and friends be there? But in a car that he'd put me in with force, going god knows where against my will? No, that never crossed my mind. The ring's huge. Three carats, at least. It's a princess cut with diamonds covering the entire band. I set it back in the case before zipping it back into the bag.

Paul watches me, the anger and frustration seething from him. "Put it on," he demands.

My blood boils as I'm consumed with rage. "Paul, you will never be my boyfriend, fiance, or husband—not then, not now, not ever. You broke me down, manipulated me, gaslighted me, and laid your hands on me like I was nothing." My voice breaks as I struggle to get out all it is I have to say to him. "You are my living, breathing nightmare. You don't deserve a single piece of me, and I fucking hope you drown in the misery you created."

Paul clenches his jaw and I know by the all too familiar look in his eyes, I've awakened the monster. Paul's hand yanks the back of my hair, then everything goes dark.

My eyes slowly open and I hear the faint sound of music playing through the ringing in my ears. I touch my hand to my pulsating forehead, realizing they're handcuffed. Blood covers my fingertips and I can only assume the pulsing in my head is from him smashing it into the dashboard after not liking my answer to his proposal.

I let out a groan in pain. He thinks that I'll just come home to him, wear his ring, and everything will be forgiven.

Fuck him.

My vision is blurred, and I know from experience I have a concussion. Where is Knox? I need him. I need him now more than ever. Head between my legs, I run my hand down the inside of my boot, trying to locate my phone while the handcuffs chatter.

"Looking for this?" Paul says, holding my phone up. Opening my eyes wider, I see the name light up my phone.

Knox.

"Who the fuck is this, Haylee?" he yells, shoving the phone in my face as Knox's name disappears and reappears with another incoming call. The corners of Paul's mouth pull up into a sadistic smile.

Paul clicks the answer button and puts the call on speaker, revealing Knox's panicked voice. "Haylee, Haylee, honey, I've got you."

Paul interrupts him before I can speak, my head still foggy from the hit. "Who the fuck is this?"

"I'm right behind you. I've got you. You hear me? I've got you." He doesn't know if I can hear him or not, but the fact he's just blatantly ignoring Paul gives me a sense of satisfaction. *Fuck you, Paul.*

As much pain as I'm in right now, the comfort of Knox courses through me, spreading a crazed smile across my face. *I love him.*

"Your little fucking whore is dead, asshole!" Paul screams into the phone, banging it against the wheel.

"I love you, Knox," I say, past the loud ring still in my ears.

Paul's face takes on a demonic form as he ends the call and reaches toward his back with one hand still on the wheel. He's going to shoot me right where he proposed to me.

I guess some might say that's some type of dark romance right there, but I'll be damned if I go out like that.

I hug my knees to my chest, gripping my shins as the handcuffs bite into me. Paul cocks the gun, pointing it toward me as he takes his attention from the road. I summon all my strength, lifting my feet off the seat, and pulling my legs back as far as I can—then I kick. I kick with everything I've got.

Chapter Twenty-Four

Knox

The line disconnects and my foot presses harder on the gas, following behind the black SUV. All I can think about is that I didn't get to tell her I love her back.

I love her.

I fucking love this woman.

I hear a familiar sound of a gunshot piercing the air and, simultaneously, the SUV Haylee occupies jolts to the left across the median and into oncoming traffic. Dread consumes my body, watching the car flip over and over again until it hits the embankment.

I slam on my brakes, pulling into the middle of the median on the highway. I jump out and hear Nik following close behind. Cars come to a halt as they come up on the crash. I sprint across the highway, paying no regard for traffic as I make my way to Haylee on the passenger side of the SUV. I pull at the mangled door, trying to get to her. She's unconscious, blood pouring from her head, her legs pinned against the collapsed dashboard.

"Call 911," I hear Nik scream at bystanders.

"Fucking come help me," I yell back. I can't even recognize my own voice. I glance over at Paul as I pull at the door with Nik. He's soaked in blood and his face is unrecognizable. I can see pieces from a glass bottle pierced through his throat.

Easy way out, you piece of shit.

Animalistic noises escape me as I pull at the door. I finally open it enough to get a part of my body in right as Haylee comes to. Her eyes meet mine before falling shut again. "I love you, Haylee."

I fucking love her. Always will. I love the way her feet are always cold, those tiny short shorts she wears, the way she belts out songs without knowing all the lyrics. I love how she loves, so deeply and without apology. Her honey-soaked eyes, her fucked up past, and the way she still is impossibly sexy even when she swears like a trucker. I love every flawed, beautiful piece of her that makes her who she is.

My eyes inspect her body for injuries. She has face lacerations, bruising, likely a broken leg, no gunshot wounds. I let out a deep breath as my hand holds the side of her face, keeping her spine straight until an ambulance can clear her to move. She blinks her eyes open a few more times. "I know it hurts right now, but you're doing so well, Haylee. You hear me? You're safe. I've got you now. I'm not going to let anything happen to you." As if she realizes where she is, she begins to panic, trying to turn her head to locate Paul.

"Haylee. Honey. Shh . . . shh . . . Haylee, focus on me. Look at me, Haylee. I've got you. I don't want you to look over there. I need you to trust me. You're safe now and I have you." She just slightly nods her head. "Now listen to me, Haylee. This is important. I do not want you to look over there. Do you understand me? He's not going to hurt you. I promise you he will never be able to hurt you again. But I need you to promise you're not going to look at him." She tries to nod again, but my hands hold her head in place as her tears paint my hand.

She may feel relief seeing Paul dead in the seat beside her, but she can see him dead in a casket. Not like this. I gain a small trace of satisfaction at his face matching the true evil that laid beneath the surface. She doesn't need to live with the gruesome images of him right now, haunting her dreams. I know what those images can do to a person and plan to protect her from it. Even if she hates him now, she loved him at one point.

I wish he didn't get such an easy way out. I'd love to know he was suffering and rotting in prison, but I know she'd still always fear the possibilities of what if. I rub my thumb across her cheek. "Shh . . . I'm here. I'm here, honey. I've got you."

I place my hands on the countertop and lean my head between my arms, taking a deep breath, releasing the pain radiating up my leg as I exhale out. "What do you think you're doing?" Knox says, walking down the stairs of his childhood home.

He runs a towel through his freshly showered hair before throwing it over the banister and making his way to me. "Making you coffee," I say, quickly pulling a smile to my face and standing upright.

The past month, Knox has done nothing but prove to me the man I knew him to be. After the car accident with Paul, I was in the hospital for two weeks. Besides a grade three concussion from my head being cracked into the dashboard, I also had a broken femur and some bleeding from my spleen. Knox never left my side. He held my hand when they rolled me away for my surgery and again when I called my parents to let them know I had been in an accident. When he left to go home just for a shower, he'd come back with a book from home or my favorite USMC sweatshirt of his. Not once did he hesitate when the pain medicine made me sick or I needed help in the bathroom. This only further proved that this man is one of a kind.

Knox comes to stand behind me, kissing the side of my neck as I lean into his touch. "Thank you, honey, but you know you're not supposed to be up without your crutches. You're in pain. Go sit." He kisses me again, this time on my cheek. Damn this man for reading me like a book.

I know I just had major surgery and my femur is now held together by rods and pins, but I am not someone who can just sit and waste away. Alyssa had offered to help nurse me back to health once I got home from the hospital, but Nik didn't think it was smart for a pregnant woman to take on that responsibility. I insisted I was fine and I could get a nurse through my insurance, but Knox said it wasn't anything he couldn't handle.

The cabin on the property would have sufficed just fine, but he insisted that his childhood home would be much better for the wheelchair I was in for the first week home.

Sitting at the U shaped couch that I've done an excellent job of breaking in, I reach toward my stack of books on the coffee table. My eye catches on my notebook, the one I'd written my bucket list in on the first day I met Knox. I grab my pen and move down the list, checking off the things I've accomplished over the past few months.

Haylee's Bucket List!

- Sing Karaoke ✓
- Swim in a lake ✓
- Run a marathon
- Ride a horse ✓
- Go camping ✓
- Join a book club
- Build a home
- Get married
- Start a family
- Change a tire ✓
- Be brave ✓

H + K

I smile, checking off the last box. I never have been truly proud of myself. I've never felt like I had accomplished anything to be proud of. I mean, I graduated high school and college, I've volunteered here and there, but my parents always made me think those aren't things to take pride in, it's just something we simply do. But overcoming the mental and physical abuse from Paul, and keeping my sister from harm's way while confronting my abuser? Yeah, I'm fucking proud of myself for that. I was brave. I was dauntless. For that, I'm finally proud of who I have become as a woman.

Knox looks at me curiously, making his way to me with two cups of coffee. "What do you have there?"

"Remember my bucket list?" I prop my leg up on the ottoman and I hand him my notebook as I snuggle into his chest and he wraps an arm around me, skimming over the list. "I started it the day you picked me up from the airport," I say matter-of-factly.

"I almost left you there, ya know?" Knox shoots back.

I lift my head up, my hand pressing into his chest, my mouth gaping at him in shock. "Excuse me? You would've just left me there?" I laugh.

"Well, I did wait a long time for you," he argues, his bright smile making its way closer before planting a kiss on my shoulder.

"Yes, well, I've waited *years* for you, Knox."

His lips brush mine, kissing me like we have all the time in the world.

Our kiss breaks and he taps the journal still in my lap. "There's one more here that I think we can cross off."

"Oh yeah, what one?" I look back down at my list to see what I've missed.

He takes the pen from the table and butterflies fill my stomach as he moves his hand down the list. He makes a check next to build a home, and I scrunch my eyebrows at him in confusion.

"You've been the one who made this house a home. You, Haylee, are what makes me feel at home. Live here. Live here with me. Make this house *our* home."

He kisses my forehead and his eyes search mine, my face lighting up at his proposal. I've been worried about how I will go back to living with Alyssa after my recovery. Not only because I'll be intruding on them being new parents, but I'll miss Knox. Spending every morning watching the sunrise while we drink our coffees, nights spent on the deck reading, cuddled under a blanket, having someone go out to pick up the pizza when I've burned dinner.

There's a quiet kind of peace in being here with him, like everything's finally in place. I spent my whole life wanting to escape—first from my parents' house, then from the one I shared with Paul. Home was always a place I longed to leave. But here, in this house with Knox, is the only one that has ever come close to feeling like a home.

"Yes, Knox. Yes, of course I'll live here with you."

Epilogue
Knox & Haylee

KNOX

Haylee looks up at the horse-drawn carriage, then back down at her bulging belly, figuring out how to get in the carriage. She's eight months pregnant and I can't say I'm surprised. We never did get around to getting those condoms.

Not that I minded.

We may have moved quicker than most, and backward if you asked her parents, but I couldn't be happier or more sure of anything. I run my hand over her stomach and reach for her hand to help her up. Even getting off the couch exerts all her energy these days.

I have a plan, though, and it'll all be worth it. Since the moment she asked what I thought about naming our baby boy after Chris, I've been planning this. Only two more things to cross off her bucket list. During her recovery, she joined a book club, then after months of physical therapy, she worked her ass off to run a 5K. Marry a good man. That's all that's left.

I originally thought of planning this in the morning at

sunrise, but unfortunately, her morning sickness never went away. I thought better of it. I'd not rather have anything interfere with my proposal. So a sunset carriage ride it was.

It's the same exact ring from the day we went to the farmers market. The way her eyes lit up when she saw it, the feeling I got in my chest when I saw it on her finger. I knew I wanted her to have it, but I wasn't sure how I would ever give it to her. The day I bought it, I could never have imagined I would be using it to propose. I had it custom altered to add a massive diamond beneath the sunburst. It's the perfect ring for her. Now, all I need is for her to say yes.

HAYLEE

I look down at my outfit, letting out a laugh. If you told me I'd be walking out of a job interview with cowgirl boots and a dress on, I'd have laughed in your face. I am no longer the woman someone else is forcing me to be. I'm just me—Haylee Hayes. That's right. He checked *every* box off my bucket list.

I knew without a doubt in my mind that Knox was the man I was going to spend my life with. A few months later, I was pregnant. Then, I was walking down the aisle toward my future husband and newborn son, Christopher.

After the accident, I used my spare time to research how I could help kids like Cade Fuller. He just so happened to get into his dream college. I used my trust fund to set the plan in motion, making sure students have access to not only afford college applications but books and housing as well. Which is what leads me here, walking out of a job interview. Being a guidance counselor isn't as glamorous or high paying as my job in the city was, but at least I can say I know it will be rewarding, and that's all I've ever wanted.

Alyssa and Nik are now expecting their second son.

Carter, their youngest, is thrilled to be a big brother and I love all the hand-me-downs for Christopher. Annabeth has easily become my best friend, and we still do karaoke from time to time.

As for Paul, there are days I feel nothing but hatred for the man he was. But then I remember—his cruelty didn't break me, it built me. Without surviving him, I wouldn't be the strong, fearless woman I am today, or have the beautiful family I cherish with everything I have.

I make my way across the street to the park, where Knox and Christopher are waiting for me. They are sitting on a blanket sharing a snack. When Knox spots me, he picks up Christopher in his arms and rushes toward me, kissing my forehead.

"How'd the interview go, honey?"

"They offered it to me on the spot."

Knox winks at me, giving me the same butterflies he did the day we first met. "They'd be idiots not to."

Acknowledgments

I still can't believe I get to say this but:

Guys, I wrote a freakin' book! And I in no way did it alone. Thank you for the ever loving support and seeing something in this mess before I did.

To Alyssa, who I mortifyingly first told I was writing a book and she gave me nothing but support to the very end.

To Bartolomeo, who let me yell at him to stop chewing so loud so I could think as I wrote—and complained.

To the Girls Room Group chat, for always giving me your brutal opinions—sorry, I still think "his beard glistened" is acceptable.

To Kelly and Christina, for reading this far too many times. I owe you both drinks.

To Joe, who sat with me in the dark parts and reminded me I could do this while I threatened to burn it to the ground.

Massive thanks to my mom and dad for making me absolutely fucked up enough in the head to write this and not be embarrassed for it.

Special thanks to Chelsea and Brittany. My fairy godmothers, my Charlie's Angels, true goddesses in every way. I couldn't have done it without your hard work. This book would forever be a Google Doc if it weren't for you two.

To the readers who took a chance on a first-time author, thank you. If you laughed, cried, or even got a little turned on, I've done my job.

Brittni DeRiggi is a debut author who came in hot and possibly a bit unhinged. She believes in broken girls, bossy men, and slow burns that end in absolute filth. When she's not writing, she is drinking ~~espresso~~ wine, reading a book, or gangster rapping to her toddler.

Brittni didn't plan to become an author, but she had a story in her head and a spicy scene she couldn't stop thinking about. With that, *Anywhere But Home* was born. Her favorite tropes are "touch her and die" and the ever loved "good girl".